"I'm the new carrier for this route," replied Austin, choosing not to be overly familiar. "I should also inform you that your. . .uh. . .mailbox here is in violation of the postal code for both size and placement near the road. Technically, we're not supposed to deliver mail into nonstandard receptacles."

Jocelyn crossed her arms and stepped back, blinking. Then, as Austin continued to stare at her, she began to smile.

"You're serious!" she exclaimed, breaking into delighted laughter and placing her hands on her tan cheeks. Austin noticed the fingernails were clipped very short, and her hands, like her legs, were too short and chunky to be considered beautiful. She ran her hands up the sides of her head, lifting her thick, tousled, badly cut, nearly black hair, then letting it fall again. "Well, here. I'll just take it from you then."

"I'm sorry, miss," Austin said solemnly, "but I feel I should also warn you that it is a federal offense to take mail that does not belong to you."

Jocelyn looked at him in disbelief. "So now you think I'm a thief, standing out here in the middle of nowhere, just waiting to rob old Wells Fargo. That's great!" She giggled again. "Well, it looks like we have us a standoff, pardner. You are one trustworthy mailman."

"Letter carrier," he said, hoping to disguise his pleasure at the somewhat oblique praise. "Do you have some identification?"

CATHERINE RUNYON makes her home in Michigan with her family. She is a news editor and columnist at the *Advance* newspaper. Catherine writes inspirational romance because she wants "to make a positive contribution" to the romance genre and to let her readers know that "though all hope seems lost, He [God] remains faithful."

Books by Catherine Runyon

HEARTSONG PRESENTS
HP178—Eagles for Anna

Prize Package

Catherine Runyon

Heartsong Presents

A note from the author:
*I love to hear from my readers! You may correspond with me
by writing:* **Catherine Runyon**
Author Relations
PO Box 719
Uhrichsville, OH 44683

ISBN 1-57748-484-3

PRIZE PACKAGE

All of the characters and events in this book are fictitious. Any
resemblance to actual persons, living or dead, or to actual events
is purely coincidental.

Cover illustration by Lauraine Bush.

PRINTED IN THE U S A

one

August

Jocelyn Wentworth rose from the straight-backed wooden chair, where she had been working since dawn, and went to the kitchen window. She rubbed at the dim, flawed glass to get a better view of what was turning out to be a glorious summer morning.

Outside the old-fashioned nine-paned wood-trimmed window, wild purple asters blanketed the edges of her property. The goldenrod were beginning to come on, and Queen Anne's lace punctuated the color scheme with white. The birds chirped lazily, their parenting work nearly done for the season. The underlying hum of crickets and cicadas so early in the day warned Jocelyn that it would be a hot afternoon. Another gorgeous day all to herself—all alone.

It has been a good morning's work, she thought, pushing away the niggling emptiness that threatened to distract her. She looked appreciatively at the pile of envelopes on the scarred table. Strewn about were opened envelopes and colorful brochures, a collection of pencils and pens, and a half-used roll of stamps. She had been reading and writing without a break for nearly four hours.

"I wonder what my teachers who called me hyperactive would say about this?" she murmured.

It suddenly occurred to her how hungry she was, and she glanced at the refrigerator, an antique with rounded corners that rattled when the compressor kicked in. This morning, however, what caught her eye was the hand-stitched sampler in shades of purple and green that hung on the wall next to the aging appliance.

"Trust in the Lord with all your heart and lean not on your own understanding," the flowing embroidered letters read. "In all your ways acknowledge him, and he will make your paths straight."

It was one of many Bible verses Aunt Bebe had left in the house in one form or another. Jocelyn vaguely remembered some of them from Sunday school, and from the times she had visited when her great-aunt still lived in this house. The verses were poetic and charming, but Jocelyn had not the slightest idea what they meant. How could anyone with a mind not trust their own understanding?

Aunt Bebe, of course, had known. Though her straightforward manner, business acumen, and industry sometimes gave people the idea she was aggressive and unfeeling, Jocelyn knew her mother's aunt to be completely at peace, and possessed of a wisdom that allowed her to know exactly when to be firm and when to bend.

If only she had not died so soon! Jocelyn thought. *I was only just beginning to appreciate her. Maybe she would have passed her secrets to me along with the house.*

Her stomach grumbled, but she decided against eating, partly because she knew there was nothing interesting in the refrigerator and partly because she did not want to take a chance on missing the mail. Energized by the thought of a chat with Whitney, the mail carrier, she grabbed the stack of envelopes, quickly riffled through them to make sure all stamps were in place, and headed out the front door.

≈

As he tooled down Greenwood Road, Austin Van Doran could just make out the shape of a person standing beside the next mailbox on his route. The mid-morning August sun reflected from the old, broken blacktop, making the shadows dance. He squinted as he slowed and pulled to the right, the tires of the U.S. Postal Service Jeep raising dust from the gravel shoulder.

Another impatient kid, he thought, noting how the girl shifted from one bare foot to the other next to the huge mailbox, the biggest he had ever seen. It was made from a twenty-gallon aluminum garbage can supported on a tripod of landscape timbers. The lid had been anchored with screws, and a square door cut into the lid and attached with a hinge.

The girl wore ragged cutoff jeans and a sweatshirt with the arms ripped out. The once-bright college logo on the front had faded to oblivion. He rolled to a stop, and she peered at him through the open side of the truck.

"Where's Whitney?" she asked, leaning inside and looking toward the back of the Jeep as though Whitney might be a hostage there. Peering from beneath wild bangs that reached nearly to her eyebrows, she stretched her neck to look beyond the boxes in the rear.

"She has been assigned to a new route," Austin answered, reaching for the next bundle on the pile of mail beside him. Then he understood why the mailbox was so large. The bundle for Jocelyn Wentworth was equal to the rest of the mail he had delivered this morning.

"I like Whitney," the girl said, obviously disappointed, and holding both her hands out for the bundle. "I was just getting used to her. Who are you?"

"I'm the new carrier for this route," replied Austin, choosing not to be overly familiar. "I should also inform you that your. . .uh. . .mailbox here is in violation of the postal code for both size and placement near the road. Technically, we're not supposed to deliver mail into nonstandard receptacles."

Jocelyn crossed her arms and stepped back, blinking. Then, as Austin continued to stare at her, she began to smile.

"You're serious!" she exclaimed, breaking into delighted laughter and placing her hands on her tan cheeks. Austin noticed the fingernails were clipped very short, and her hands, like her legs, were too short and chunky to be considered beautiful. She ran her hands up the sides of her head, lifting her thick, tousled, badly cut, nearly black hair, then letting it fall again. "Well, here. I'll just take it from you then."

"I'm sorry, miss," Austin said solemnly, "but I feel I should also warn you that it is a federal offense to take mail that does not belong to you."

Jocelyn looked at him in disbelief. "So now you think I'm a thief, standing out here in the middle of nowhere, just waiting to rob old Wells Fargo. That's great!" She giggled again. "Well, it looks like we have us a standoff, pardner. You are one trustworthy mailman."

"Letter carrier," he said, hoping to disguise his pleasure at the somewhat oblique praise. "Do you have some identification?"

"Yesiree! Stay here. I'll be right back." Before he could protest, her bare feet were gingerly hopping across the hot pavement, then springing through knee-high grass and weeds, up splintered wooden steps, and through a front door that looked like it was about to fall off.

Austin watched her bound into the ramshackle house and wondered briefly who else lived there. He noticed the car in the driveway. It was a nineteen-year-old Lincoln Continental—no doubt a showpiece at one time—that had one door a different color than the rest of the body, and a crumpled left quarter panel. He wondered if it ran.

If only a large dog were tied to the tree out front, the picture would be complete, Austin thought. He had seen his share of poor homes like this one during his travels with the Air Force. He had joined expecting to spend his time in high-tech laboratories, but instead had bounced around the back roads of Texas assisting with government surveys. No matter. The service had paid for college, his ultimate goal, and had led him into civil service, the most stable employment he could envision.

He waited impatiently, glancing often at his watch, anxious to get on with his route, which would be slow anyway because he was unfamiliar with the stops. He hated this kind of indecision, where both choices seemed wrong.

Not that her mail seemed all that important. It looked like a lot of sweepstakes entries and other junk mail. There was not a personal letter in the bundle.

"Here you go!" Jocelyn again appeared at the window, carrying two snapshots of herself. Her name was on the back of them.

Austin stared at them, then at her.

"But—this isn't identification. Don't you have something official, like a driver's license?"

"Oh, sure," she said, and pulled the card from the back pocket of her cutoffs. "It's just that the picture is so bad, nobody could tell this is me." She passed the license to Austin. "There you go. I'm Jocelyn Wentworth, just like it says."

Austin was satisfied with the likeness. He noted the birth date, and quickly calculated that she was twenty years old, as of last month. He handed back the license, and began to pass the stacks of mail to her. "You must be on every list in the country."

She nodded. "I know it's kind of a pain for you, but this is my job. I enter contests. I read every single thing that comes to me. So don't think of this as information pollution or anything like that. I really want all this stuff."

Suddenly Austin made the connection between the description the former carrier had given him and the young woman at the window. Whitney had warned him he might need a separate tub for the mail at 22 Greenwood Road, but he had thought she was exaggerating.

Jocelyn began stuffing the mail into a brown paper shopping bag.

"Not much today," she remarked. "But don't worry about it. I don't blame you."

Austin only half-stifled a cry of exasperation. He wondered whether she also blamed the weatherman for rain.

Just as he was about to put the truck in gear she called, "Hey, are you married or engaged or anything?"

He was so startled by the question that he simply answered. "No."

"My mom's having a pool party at her house tonight. Want to come?"

He stared at her. "But—you don't even know me."

"Well, maybe I'd like to know you. Come to the pool party. I'll get to know you."

As long as he lived, he would not know why he did not turn down the invitation on the spot. Something in her ingenuous approach, perhaps her simple joy in receiving the mail he so seriously labored over, or maybe just his own bleak prospects for another evening alone, made him consider.

"A pool party?"

"Yes!" she said. Her eyes were wide and she spoke louder, as if he somehow didn't understand English. "A pool party. Swimming. In the swimming pool. Eating outside. At my mother's house. With my friends."

It was all so improper, disorderly, and somehow appealing. She was tapping her foot in the gravel on the shoulder of the road, fidgeting a bit. His thoughts were whirling. Had he unintentionally sent her a message that he was attracted to her?

Suddenly she interrupted his thoughts. "What's your name?"

"Austin Van Doran."

"Classy name!" she breathed, and she seemed to sparkle. "Well, Austin, do you want to come to the party or not? I'm getting hot out here. If you need some more time to think about it, pull into the shade."

"No, I have to get on with my route. Yes. I'll go. Thank you for the invitation, though I don't know—I don't understand—well, thank you. Shall I come for you here this evening?"

"Let's just meet at my mom's place." She pulled a pencil from her pocket and wrote down the address on the back of one of the postcards that had just been delivered. "This is where she lives. I'll see you there. No alcohol. Mom doesn't allow it."

"That's fine with me," Austin said, tucking the card into his shirt pocket. "I'll see you there. Once again, thanks."

As he pulled away, Jocelyn noted that he watched her in the side mirror. She stared after him for a time, then wiggled her fingers in a good-bye wave and walked toward her house, dragging the sack full of mail.

Meanwhile, Austin's heart was racing and his mind swam. What an outrageous act he had just committed! Only one other time in his life could he remember feeling this way, and that was when he had sneaked into his parents' bedroom, stolen two quarters from his father's night table, and escaped out the window when he heard his mother coming down the hall. He had run all the way to the convenience store on the corner to buy a cold drink, out of breath, giddy, and never able to share the experience with anyone.

After a few routine stops, his mind settled, and with it his breathing and his pulse. Why had he said yes? Just because she was an attractive young woman? Well, attractive might not be the right word. Pleasant. Friendly. It seemed so good to be looking forward to an evening out with a new acquaintance. He could hardly remember the last time it had happened. The great irony of his life was that now, when he had met all the goals he considered necessary to permit him to pursue personal relationships, there weren't any. As he inched along his route, he had to admit that in spite of all his success, he was lonely, and had so far been unable to break out of the cage he had constructed for himself. Jocelyn, in a moment, had broken in.

Jocelyn went inside, dumped her bag in the middle of the floor and began quickly and efficiently sorting the contents into several piles. She was familiar by now with the offerings of promotional companies, and she knew almost instinctively which materials would be worth opening, which would have to be read carefully, and which could be handled with a standardized return postcard.

Though her eyes scanned the colorful brochures and envelopes cleverly designed to make the recipient want to open them, her thoughts were still with Austin. She had never in her life asked a man for a date, and certainly not a man she had only met minutes before. She knew she had a tendency to talk a little too much, a little too fast, and to be impulsive, but this was outside the limits even for her.

Jocelyn only knew that when she had come into the house to look for the snapshots, she had been overcome with a feeling that this man was unique. Maybe it was the way he had protected what must seem to him to be worthless junk mail. Maybe it was his voice, which poured out like warm honey, or his proper, rather shy demeanor. He was polite, purposeful, dedicated, a no-nonsense kind of person. His deep blue eyes were clear and steady. Only the neatly trimmed beard seemed incongruous to her. She had never trusted men with beards, but she was willing to make an exception now. In return for his conscientious actions, she had wanted to give him a gift. She had nothing but her friendship, and she was thrilled he had said yes.

❧

When Austin arrived at Adelle Wentworth's suburban home, he was startled to find Jocelyn had already arrived, wearing the same ragged shorts and sweatshirt he had seen her in earlier. He had spent nearly an hour selecting his outfit, trying to decide whether safari shorts were too casual, since he had never met the hostess, and whether to wear socks with loafers or to go with sandals. He had finally opted for the shorts, ironing them carefully before dressing, and compromised on dock shoes without socks.

The shirt was never in question. Only his cadet blue half-sleeve crisp cotton would do. In that shirt, he felt equal to any challenge. As he put it on, however, he wondered why he felt this pool party was a challenge. In fact, why was everything a challenge lately? He had worn this shirt so often in the past year it was like another kind of uniform.

He found the house without any problem. Being a mail carrier had its benefits. *Well,* he thought as he caught sight of his reflection in the patio doors at the Wentworth house, *no time to back out now.* Jocelyn was coming toward him.

"Austin, come and meet my mother," she cried, tugging at his sturdy forearm. She stood beside him and the top of her head reached just above his elbow. "She's having this party for me, in a way, because she thinks I never have any fun. A lot of my old friends are here, people I knew in high school who are home for the summer, mostly. Mom thinks I should have gone to college, and I wouldn't be lonely if I had. Not that I'm lonely. She thinks I am. I don't care. I love a party, so what difference does it make why we're having it?"

Austin's contribution to the conversation was simply

to listen, somewhat befuddled, to the cheerful stream of conversation.

Jocelyn pulled him toward a slender, forty-something woman whose hair was simply and elegantly cut and just beginning to gray. She was dressed in a khaki wrap skirt and a deep red blouse that was a feminine version of his shirt. Large gold hoop earrings brushed the ironed collar as she nodded attentively while listening to a guest. Austin liked her at once.

"Mom, this is Austin, the one I told you about. Don't mind the beard," Jocelyn said as soon as she could break into the conversation. "He's honest. He's the new mailman on the route. My mother, Adelle Wentworth."

"Letter carrier, actually," said Austin. He smiled and grasped Mrs. Wentworth's outstretched hand. "That's the official designation. I'm happy to meet you."

"It was so nice of you to come on the spur of the moment," Adelle said. "Jocelyn is so spontaneous, she sometimes forgets that other people plan things in advance."

"Well, I had no plans for the evening. I was glad for the invitation," replied Austin. "From the looks of the crowd, you wouldn't have missed me."

"Jocelyn is very well-liked," Adelle remarked. "She draws people. It's her gift."

Austin caught a note of something—wistfulness?—in Adelle's description of her daughter. He followed her gaze to the grill where Jocelyn stood holding a plate, waiting for the cook to take up a batch of hamburgers.

"Is that Mr. Wentworth at the grill?"

"That's our neighbor, Richard. Jocelyn's father died when she was ten."

Austin nodded, deciding no response was the best one. "Your home is lovely. It must be a lot of work for you, keeping it up all alone."

"I do only what I like," said Adelle. "A little gardening, the decorating. My husband was a good planner. I have what I need. I often hire Richard to do the heavier work I can't manage myself, or college students during the summer. Do you have your own place?"

Austin managed to control the note of pride that threatened to enter his voice.

"Yes, I was able to find a bargain after I finished college. Unlike most of my classmates, I graduated without loans to pay off. My bills were paid largely by the military college plan." He looked straight ahead, but tried to roll his eyes sideways far enough to see if she was impressed.

He was rewarded with a warm, open smile, and words of praise. "I would say you are a very levelheaded young man. Most young people are still living with their parents at your age. They're still thinking of trips to Florida in the spring and planning to get an apartment with a roommate when they graduate—*if* they can find a job. How did you get your feet so firmly on the ground?"

Austin crossed his arms and spread his feet a little. "Well, I've always had a plan for things I wanted and when—"

Jocelyn interrupted, handing Austin a plate holding a burger on a bun, lettuce and tomato, and an assortment of vegetables and dip.

"I didn't get you any potato salad," she said. "I don't eat it myself. You don't like it, do you? It's all eggs and mayonnaise with a few potatoes thrown in, loaded with fat."

"This is fine," replied Austin, accepting the plate.

"Come and sit down with me," Jocelyn said. "You know all about me and I don't know anything about you. Come and talk to me."

Austin smiled at Adelle. "We'll talk later," he promised and obediently followed after Jocelyn.

Jocelyn's plate had two hamburgers, extra tomatoes, and a heap of vegetables double the size of his. Between bites, she told him about the neighborhood and about the other people at the party.

"I grew up in this house," she explained. "It's the only place I ever lived in until I moved into Aunt Bebe's house. That's where I live now. She left it to me. She was my mother's aunt."

The dozen or so people in the pool and around it were old friends from the neighborhood, she said, people with whom she had gone to high school, people whose parents were friends of her parents.

"My mom gives great parties," she commented, and Austin thought he heard the same tone her mother had used. "She's a good person. She's not like some of those rich widows who spend their life in the beauty shop and the mall. In fact, she isn't really rich, just comfortable, you know? My dad was great to her. She doesn't know how good, really. Anyway, having people around is good for her, and good for them. People like her. You see how she charmed you."

"Strange," Austin said. "She said approximately the same thing about you."

"Oh, well, she's always polite. One thing Mom could never be accused of is losing her cool."

"I think she's wonderful, but I can't decide if you like her or not."

"She's my mother!" Jocelyn said, a little too quickly. "Of course I like her. It's just that we don't agree on everything. I suppose you agree with your mother on everything?"

Austin smiled and stared at his plate. "No."

"Mom is afraid I'm going to embarrass her by being a failure. She's hoping I'll marry somebody rich and boring who'll settle me down, but I won't. I don't want the kind of life she has."

"Was your father rich and boring?"

"My father was great," she said, starting on the second burger. "What did she tell you about him?"

"Just that he died when you were ten."

"He was great," Jocelyn said again. They ate in silence for a moment, then she brushed crumbs off her lap, tossed the paper plate into the trash, stood up, and said, "I'm going swimming. What about you?"

"Go ahead," said Austin. "I'll get my bag from the car and change." Then, as he was finishing his last bite of burger, Jocelyn ran and jumped into the pool, clothes and all.

Austin laughed out loud, half in surprise, half in embarrassment. He caught sight of Adelle, whose face registered mild exasperation as she watched her daughter, but then she turned back to the guest to whom she was speaking as if nothing unusual had happened.

Jocelyn played in the pool a while, apparently at ease with all the people in the group. Then she climbed out, water pouring from her clothing. She walked toward Austin, who still stood at the edge of the lawn. He instinctively recoiled as she approached. When Jocelyn was right next to him she shook her hair.

"Come on, Austin. This is a pool party," she said.

"Yes, I know. I was just on my way to change."

Adelle was suddenly next to them. "Jocelyn, would you join me in the house a moment?"

"No, I'm wet and I'll drip all over. What do you want?"

Adelle lowered her voice, though her proximity to Austin prohibited privacy. "Most of the people here are familiar with your teasing, Jocelyn, but I'm sure Austin is not."

"We're just getting to know each other," Jocelyn said, her voice steady. "Don't worry about me, Mother, and don't apologize for my behavior. I'm an adult. No one blames you for me anymore."

Adelle seemed to Austin to be infinitely patient. "I'm only hoping to save you from unpleasant memories. Tomorrow, you will feel quite differently than you do now."

"You make me sound like an old drunk," said Jocelyn, and Austin wished he were somewhere else. He excused himself, though neither woman noticed, and walked toward the pool. He was about to quietly exit and pretend he had never met Jocelyn Wentworth when he heard her say just a little bit too loudly, "He came to be with me, Mother, not to be inspected by you."

Austin could not hear Adelle's response, but Jocelyn came through loud and clear, "I've been here for two hours, Mother. I'm ready to leave. I'm sure Austin is, too."

Adelle followed her daughter toward Austin, saying, "I know I can't change your mind, Jocelyn. I'm only asking that you spend some time, out of courtesy, with some of your old friends who have come from out of town, those who just arrived."

Austin felt a familiar tightness in his chest, a feeling

that always came over him when he heard people arguing. He had to stop it.

"Jocelyn, I'd be happy to stay a while," said Austin. It seemed the most natural thing in the world for him to sacrifice his own comfort to settle this dispute. "Don't feel you have to spend the evening with me. Your friends are my friends."

Others had begun to notice the dispute and were casting surreptitious glances in the direction of Jocelyn and Adelle. Jocelyn's wet hair was pasted over her eyes. Her baggy clothing now hung down at the sides, and her mouth was tight with anger.

"I knew it," Jocelyn muttered. "He got to you, didn't he? Is it the beard, Mom? Is that why you think he's so great?" Turning to Austin, she said sarcastically, "Mom thinks you're the one who'll normalize me, Austin."

"Jocelyn!" Adelle cried. "I said nothing about Austin. We've only just met. Please, don't embarrass yourself and us. You know this isn't what you wanted to have happen this evening."

"Well, you're right about that," said Jocelyn. "I was hoping for a nice time."

Austin smiled his brightest, and placed one hand on Jocelyn's soggy shoulder, one on Adelle's crisp shoulder. "We are having a pleasant evening. The food is great, the people here are all friends. I'm going to go change and have a swim. Will you join me, Jocelyn?"

"I was right about not trusting a man with a beard," said Jocelyn flatly. "I'm going home. Enjoy the pool." And with a sudden thrust, she pushed him in.

two

September

The purple loosestrife in the wetlands along Greenwood Road was fading to pale heather. The sun was a little lower in the sky each day as Austin turned the corner from Pardee Drive. He hardly needed to have the sun visor down anymore. Summer would soon be over.

He went methodically from mailbox to mailbox. For the first time he considered the relationship between "route" and "routine," and wondered if security was going to be as wonderful as he had anticipated. It was what he had wanted all his life. Now he realized it came with a big side dish of boredom.

Perhaps the work would be less onerous if he had continued to see Jocelyn at the mailbox as he had that first day, three weeks ago. He often imagined her scampering from the house, fidgeting at the side of the mailbox, or waving to him as she had that day. Why her image continued to haunt him he could not explain. After her deplorable behavior, he knew he should put her out of his mind completely, but he could not.

He had not spoken to Jocelyn since the night of the pool party. Though he had seen her peeking through the curtains a couple of times as he approached, she always pulled them shut before he got to the box, and did not come out to meet him. The more he thought about the night of the party, the less he knew what he would say if he ever saw her again.

"Oh, I'm sure it was unintentional," he had rehearsed the day after she pushed him into the pool. The college crowd at the party had thought it quite a joke, and someone had pulled him back in as he tried to climb up the ladder. When he finally got out, Jocelyn was gone. He had heard the old Lincoln roar to life in the driveway and knew that he would have no opportunity to talk to her. Adelle had only offered him a deeply sorrowful glance, a slight shake of her head, and a small, almost imperceptible gesture of the hands.

"Don't worry," he rehearsed when a week had passed and she had not appeared to apologize. "There's no harm done." His favorite shirt was ruined. He had lost every shred of dignity when, as he tried to move away from the group quietly, the girls in the pool had draped a spare swimsuit top over his head.

After two weeks, he had stopped rehearsing any lines at all, deciding Jocelyn had had her fun and was now telling the story to her many friends at his expense. That was the week he refused to look at the window as he drove to the house and convinced himself that even if he ever did see her again, he would be nothing but professional. It was time to maintain control and forget the whole episode. Jocelyn was obviously not a person who was under control; therefore, she must be avoided.

Yet each day as the leaves on the willows seemed a little more transparent and the goldenrod turned dusty and peppered the pavement along Greenwood Road with pollen, he thought of her and how she had looked—grinning at him with arms flung wide—as she invited him to jump into the pool with her. Some secret part of him had longed to join in her fun, and to somehow draw her into his silent, solitary life.

The faint squeal of his brakes pulled his thoughts away from Jocelyn and reminded him to put in a request for maintenance on the truck. As he reached for the mailbox, he noticed a boy and a girl playing in the yard, which sloped sharply upward toward the house. He had not seen children here before and thought it was odd they were not in school. They did not look sick, and he knew it was not a vacation day. The buses had been passing him as usual.

The little boy ran toward the road, but stopped abruptly. Austin saw the front door of the house open a crack and assumed someone had warned the child away from the truck. Good! Children were not only a nuisance, but a hazard. They threw rocks and sticks and dirt, and lost mail on the way to the house. Usually the carrier took the blame. Children might be all right if they were disciplined, but he kept a wary eye on these two.

The little girl posed no threat. She seemed frail, and her large, bright eyes gave her an air of vulnerability. The boy took her hand and led her toward the house, glancing back over his shoulder at Austin.

Austin had one more stop before Jocelyn's shiny garbage can mailbox came into view—not long enough to prepare. Since the beginning of the route, he knew he would see Jocelyn today. He took a deep breath as he made the turn into the gravel driveway and stopped beside Jocelyn's car. He exhaled sharply as he gathered up her mail, including the certified letter for which her signature was required, and walked toward the front door. At the top of the dilapidated steps, he knocked on the shabby door. There was a slight movement at the curtain, then Jocelyn flung the door open wide.

"I knew you'd come eventually," she said, smiling. "Come in! I made some cookies."

Austin glanced self-consciously at Jocelyn. She was wearing the same shorts and sweatshirt as the day he met her. Her tan was deeper, emphasizing even more her white teeth and dark eyes. Her hair was in slight disarray, but even as she stood in the darkened interior of her home, the light from the doorway seemed to seek out the dark, soft waves and make them glow. Her bangs were even longer now, covering her eyebrows. Austin had to force himself not to reach out and brush them away from her face.

"Certified mail," he croaked, then cleared his throat and tried again. "Sign here for special delivery," he said, holding out a clipboard with one hand while balancing the load of mail in the other.

"Oh, good, that means money," said Jocelyn, quickly scribbling her name. "Can't you come in?"

He shook his head. "Sorry, I'm working." He stood looking at her for a moment, then blurted out a completely unrehearsed line. "I'm sorry I didn't get to say good-bye at the party."

As soon as he said it, he knew it was the right thing to say. All the mild reproaches he had imagined and the hypothetical conversations he had played and replayed in his mind had seemed inadequate. The thing that had hurt him the most that night was that she had left without him, and he thought he might never be able to talk to her again.

"We didn't get off to such a good start," Austin said. "Maybe we could start over."

"I start over every single day," she replied. "Just one cookie?"

He gave a quick nod of his head as she took the mail from him and he felt her cool, smooth hand brush his own. He stepped inside the house, his eyes growing accustomed to the dim light. *Perhaps now that we've made up,* he thought, *she'll open the curtains once again.*

As he looked around, however, he thought maybe it would be best if this place never saw the light of day. On every flat surface there were piles of mail, the kind of third-rate stuff he delivered every day. He noticed letters and cards and brochures, not strewn about, but piled up to six inches high on the coffee table, the arms of the sofa, the floor, windowsills, and on top of a lamp. Pencils and pens of all shapes and varieties lay among the piles. Jelly jars, plastic cups, and mismatched Tupperware—half-full of some dark liquid—dotted the living room.

The draperies at the three windows he passed did not match each other or the few pieces of furniture. The narrow hallways were further constricted by an accumulation of things—an open, empty guitar case, some books and magazines, stereo speakers apparently unconnected to any sound system, a floor lamp without a shade, a tennis racket with the wrappings hanging loose. Austin knew he wanted to see more of Jocelyn, but not of her house.

Austin sat at the table in Jocelyn's kitchen. The room was as much an eyesore to him as the rest of her house. He ate one of the rather tasteless cookies and drank half a cup of very good coffee.

"This coffee is excellent," he commented.

"Makes up for the cookies, right?" Jocelyn asked, biting into one. "They're pretty bad. I'm not much of a cook. I have this great coffeemaker, though. I won it in a drawing at the market where I shop. I entered my name 114 times. I also got about half a ton of coffee in little packets. I probably should have waited to make the cookies until I had as much sugar as the recipe called for. I'm out of sugar."

Ordinarily, Austin would have been embarrassed by such a frank admission of ineptitude, but he was forced to smile. What kind of person started baking cookies knowing she was short of the main ingredient?

"This recipe called for peanut butter," Jocelyn continued, "but I didn't have any peanut butter either, so I put in some coconut and an extra egg. You never know. I've made some great cookies just messing around with recipes. These are not some of them."

Austin wanted to ask her why she had pushed him into the pool, but he had already suggested that they start over, and that settled it. She was clearly impulsive and she had obviously been angry. She wasn't about to push her mother into the pool, but he had been a convenient alternative. If it had made her feel better, then his mission as peacemaker had been accomplished.

"I just want to say I'm sorry for pushing you into the pool," she said all in a rush when he raised his cup to finish the last of his coffee. "But I was mad at my mother, and I couldn't very well push her in, could I?"

He stared at her, startled by the uncanny mirroring of his thoughts. He took in the half-defiant, half-pleading tone of her voice and the expectant look on her face.

"I understand," he said. "Jocelyn, will you have dinner with me this evening? I'd like to take you to the Inn on the River. It's one of my favorite places. I want to go while the weather is still warm and we can sit outside by the water."

"Yes! I'd love it! Come and pick me up. If I drive my old wreck over there, the security people will run me off."

Austin tried not to stare at the surroundings as he left the house, and he was thankful to be back into his well-ordered truck. He did not see Jocelyn watching him through the kitchen window, or the sadness in her expression. When he was out of sight, Jocelyn left the house and walked east on Greenwood to her friend's home to make a phone call.

When Austin returned to the post office at the end of the day, his supervisor, Mary Ellen, stopped him.

"There was a call for you from Jocelyn Wentworth. Said she can't go this evening. Is that Jocelyn on Greenwood? The one that gets all the junk mail?"

"I thought the mail was supposed to be private," said Austin.

"Everybody knows Jocelyn," commented Mary Ellen. "She's a real nut case, but cute. Everybody likes her. Hmmm! I would never have put you two together."

"We're not together," he snapped, and turned away, refusing to acknowledge the sly smile spreading across Mary Ellen's face.

Austin's temper simmered as he finished his afternoon responsibilities and started home. When he found himself exceeding the speed limit, he knew he had to get back in control. There could be any number of reasons why Jocelyn canceled their date. Maybe she had become ill from the cookies. Maybe there was a family emergency. What did he know about her, really? He didn't even know her phone number.

When he got home, he looked for her name in the phone book, but found only her mother's number. He decided not to call Mrs. Wentworth and risk needless alarm. As he thought about it, he did not remember seeing a phone in Jocelyn's house. Of course, that didn't mean it wasn't there, buried.

Austin went outside to work in his small, neat yard, pruning the fading foliage of the summer annuals and preparing beds for the hardy mums he would soon plant. His work was interrupted by the telephone, and he quickly jumped up and ran to make sure he didn't miss what he was sure would be Jocelyn's call.

"This is Austin Van Doran," he said, trying not to sound breathless.

"Hi, Austin, it's Dad. Are you busy?"

"The usual," said Austin, hoping his disappointment was not too obvious.

"How about coming over tomorrow evening?" asked Martin Van Doran. "You can help me get the yard in shape. You're so good at it. I'll cook for you. How about it? I haven't seen you since you started your new job."

"Sure, Dad. I'll be over after work. Are your tools in good shape?"

There was a pause, then Martin admitted, "I haven't been in the shed for some time. Maybe you'd be more comfortable using your own things."

Austin knew what he would find in his father's shed. Shovels pitted with rust because they had been put away with soil clinging to them, rakes with broken handles, and a wheelbarrow with a flat tire. *He's as careless with his property as he was with his family,* Austin thought.

They spoke briefly about what kind of work needed to be done, and Austin suddenly had an idea. "I might bring someone—a new friend," he said. "She's very friendly and cheerful. You'll enjoy her company, I believe."

"Bring her along. The more the merrier."

The next day Austin found Jocelyn waiting for him at the mailbox.

"Sorry about last night," she apologized. "Something came up."

They chatted for a few moments, but Austin said nothing about his plans for the evening. He gathered from her comments that her evening was open, then he drove on.

After his shift, he went home, changed into sneakers, jeans, and a sweatshirt, and drove his white Chevy Cavalier back to Jocelyn's house.

When Jocelyn heard a car pull into her driveway, she had no idea who to expect. When she saw Austin get out and approach the house, she jumped up from the sofa where she had been working and ran to meet him.

"Hi!" she exclaimed, throwing open the door. "What are you doing here? What a pretty car."

"I'm on my way to do some yardwork at my dad's place. He's cooking dinner. Would you like to come along?"

"Sure! Just let me put my shoes on," she said. She still wore the same short-sleeved sweatshirt. Austin could now discern the logo was Georgia State University. Instead of cutoff denim shorts, she was wearing faded sweatpants. The knitted cuffs were stretched and threadbare above Jocelyn's bare feet. She turned quickly and scampered away, leaving Austin on the front step. In a moment she was back wearing the sweatshirt, comfortable-looking jeans, and worn but good quality leather sandals.

Martin Van Doran lived only a short distance from Jocelyn's house, but along the way an invisible line between semirural homes and suburban homes was crossed. Jocelyn talked pleasantly on the way, pointing out to Austin landscape features she thought interesting or pretty, and calling his attention to homes and yards she especially liked. He was comfortable with her, and grateful that she did not offer heavy conversation that demanded interaction. In fact, he was feeling some sense of pride that he had actually managed this successful rendezvous.

Austin's father was outside when they arrived.

"Dad, this is Jocelyn Wentworth. Jocelyn, my father, Martin Van Doran."

Jocelyn reached to shake Martin's hand. "Hi, Mr. Van Doran."

"Hi, Jocelyn," he said. "Would you like to help me test my new game?"

"Sure. How do you play?"

"Dad, what about the yardwork?" Austin protested as the two started to move away.

"Oh, go right ahead!" said Martin. "You know where the tools are." Suddenly, he turned to Jocelyn. "Unless you'd rather be with Austin. He's going to whip my yard into shape."

"I want to see the game first," Jocelyn said. "Did you buy it or is it a gift or what?"

"Oh, I didn't buy it. I invented it. That's what I do. I invent games and then try to convince companies to produce and sell them."

"Oh, what fun!" exclaimed Jocelyn. "What have you invented?"

"Well, let's see. My biggest success was June and January, a card game where the loser gets stuck marrying someone three times their age, or else paying for a daughter's expensive wedding, or some other bad thing."

"You invented that game? My girlfriends and I used to play it when I was a kid! We used to laugh at the pictures of the cranky old men and wrinkled old maids. And you had such funny names for them! I had to marry Lobellio Lozenge once. My favorite wedding card was the one where the father had to pay for the whole party to climb to the top of Mt. Everest for the ceremony. It was just the kind of thing a little girl could imagine."

"Well, that's high praise!" said Martin. "Let's see how you like this one." He handed her a device like a pencil with a pull string wrapped around it and a circular plastic attachment like a helicopter blade. She pulled the string and the disc flew skyward.

"This is old," she said, disappointed. "You can get these anywhere."

"Watch a minute," Martin said. As the disc began its descent, bubbles began flowing from the center. Jocelyn clapped her hands in glee.

"How did you do that?" she asked. "I didn't notice any liquid when I launched it."

"It's inside, and the change in air direction opens a little valve that lets the bubbles form and escape. The problem is that it doesn't always work. You'll love the bubbles, though. Just wait." As the bubbles floated to the ground, they did not break. They landed on the grass and stayed round and whole, gradually becoming more and more iridescent until they finally dried and popped.

"That's wonderful," Jocelyn said. "Regular soap bubbles break the second they touch the grass."

"I changed the recipe a bit using a liquid polymer," explained Martin. "They won't hold that way everywhere, because some grasses are so sharp they simply puncture the bubble. On a typical suburban lawn, though, a pretty good percentage will land whole. The beauty of this is that kids have to keep buying more bubble liquid all the time. Any toy with a consumable attached is a plus for the retailer."

Meanwhile, Austin had dragged out tools and had begun spading the borders around the garage, pulling the summer weeds and dead annuals, and watering the few hardy plants that remained. He wondered if the lawn mower would work, whether his father had ever replaced the spark plug that had burned out the last time Austin had used the mower. Austin hoped none of the neighbors thought he still lived here. It was the worst-looking yard on the block.

As he worked, he watched his father and Jocelyn enjoying themselves. It seemed it was always this way. He took care of the things that were necessary, and his father had fun. While he was still in high school, Austin had decided that was the reason his mother had left. She just couldn't put up with Martin's childishness anymore. Austin had made himself a promise that he would live differently, but he could not bring himself to abandon his father to his irresponsible ways.

The yard was small, and after two hours Austin began putting the tools away. Martin and Jocelyn were no longer in the yard. Austin repaired the lawn mower but did not start cutting the grass. That, he decided, he would leave for his dad. He went into the kitchen, washed his hands, and then lifted the lid on the pot roast simmering in the small electric roaster on the kitchen counter. He had to admit his father had a way with food. Austin got out plates and set the table, then mixed a pitcher of lemonade. Then he went to the basement where his father did his work.

Jocelyn and Martin had their heads together, bent over the new toy.

"What if it were metal?" Jocelyn was asking.

Martin shook his head. "Any extra weight, and it will tip. Then it just falls without releasing. I'm wondering if the liquid is too thick. Maybe the batches I've made haven't been consistent."

"Looks like the pot roast is done," said Austin, "and I'm starved. Are either of you interested in eating?"

They looked at him as though he were an uninvited stranger. "Austin!" Jocelyn exclaimed. "Oh, I'm so sorry! You've been working and working while we played."

Austin felt completely righteous and vindicated. She had recognized his sacrifice. "It's all right," he said. "I don't mind."

Martin whispered conspiratorially, "Austin is very good at yardwork. He has the personality for it. He's patient and thorough, but he hasn't learned to enjoy doing what he does well. You keep after him. Maybe he'll figure it out."

Before Austin could protest, Martin laid down the tiny screwdriver he held and said, "Let's go upstairs. We'll figure this out eventually, probably when we aren't even thinking about it. That's usually what happens."

Austin watched in silence as the pair walked up the stairs still chatting. He felt as if he were the butler.

When dinner was over and they had said their good-byes, Jocelyn and Austin got back into his car. Martin stood on the porch and watched them go. Jocelyn waved as they pulled away.

"Your dad is a great guy," said Jocelyn.

"Sometimes," Austin replied.

She punched him lightly on the shoulder. "Oh, don't be such a stick in the mud," she said. "He is a great guy! You're allowed to say that. It doesn't mean you aren't a man if you admit you like your dad."

"So now you practice psychology as well as the culinary arts," said Austin.

"No, but anyone can see you don't really approve of him. Why not? He's loads of fun. Didn't you have a wonderful time playing with his games and toys when you were growing up?"

"I didn't play. I was busy taking care of the yard."

"Oh, what a grump," teased Jocelyn. "You need professional help. Write yourself a letter and tell yourself to have a little fun once in a while. Better yet, listen to your dad. Learn to enjoy the work you're good at, and it will be fun for you."

Austin simply shook his head slightly and offered a wry smile.

"Oh, come on!" Jocelyn said, with no hint of anger or condemnation in her voice. "Tell me you didn't enjoy sprucing up your dad's yard. It looks beautiful after only a couple of hours under your care. Don't ruin it by making it seem like drudgery. You have a gift. You can use it to make people happy."

Austin knew she was right, and he knew his father was right. It might have been easier to accept Jocelyn's advice had it not also come from his father.

"I'll think about it," he said. "You're right, I do get a great sense of accomplishment from gardening. I just don't know that I ever thought of it as fun."

There was a moment of quiet and then Austin said, "Jocelyn, why did you cancel our dinner date?"

She turned away from him. "It's complicated."

She's seeing someone else, Austin thought. But why wouldn't she be? She was probably seeing plenty of other men—men who laughed and joked and talked about things other than their job at the post office, men who were witty and spontaneous and exuberant like her.

"Well, all right, I'll tell you," she said suddenly, just as he decided not to ask her again. "I agreed to go with you because I wanted to go so much, but as soon as the words were out of my mouth, I knew I couldn't go. I just didn't have the guts to tell you to your face. I—well, do you like my sweatshirt?" She grabbed the front, pulled it away from her body and looked down at it.

Austin shrugged, confused. "I guess it's all right."

"It's a rag," she said, "but the truth is, when I left home last spring, I sold my clothes because I needed the money. I don't have any good clothes at all."

Austin had no idea what to say. This might be the only woman in the county who really and truly did not have anything to wear!

"That's why I was so glad when you came back this afternoon. I wanted so much to be with you, and I was afraid you might never ask me again after—"

"I was beginning to think my father had stolen you away," Austin said quietly, turning into her driveway.

"He's a little old, but at least he doesn't have a beard," Jocelyn said. "And he makes a great pot roast." Austin remembered Jocelyn had eaten three servings.

"Jocelyn—" he started, but could not think of anything else. What should he say? Should he ask her not to go back into her wilderness of a house, leaving him in his neat little world in the car? Should he ask her to go out with him again? Where?

"I tried to call you," he continued. "I couldn't find your phone number. The operator said it had been disconnected. Is your phone out of order? That's not safe when you live alone."

"I don't have a phone right now," she said. "I'll see you tomorrow. We can talk then."

"Tomorrow's my day off," he said.

"Better yet. Come and pick me up. We'll go fishing."

He frowned. "Fishing? I haven't been fishing since I was ten."

"I've got poles and everything," said Jocelyn. "They were my father's. We used to go fishing a lot."

Austin tipped his head to one side. "You sold your clothes, but kept your fishing gear?"

Jocelyn grinned. "Just a matter of priorities."

"When should I come?"

"Whenever. I'm not going anywhere without you."

He let the words echo in his brain, then looked directly into her eyes, and slowly reached one hand toward her face, pushing the hair away as he had been longing to do for days. The pale softness of her forehead offset the freckles on her tan cheeks. Her dark brown eyes framed by thick black lashes ended the little-girl look. She seemed older, more sophisticated, certainly more alluring.

"I'll see you in the morning," he said, letting his hand fall to her shoulder. He could not stop looking at her eyes. She smiled, nodded, and opened the car door. "Don't bother to shave," she said, and ran into the house.

three

October

"Social Security day," said Mary Ellen as Austin loaded his truck. "They'll be waiting at the boxes for their checks."

Austin nodded. "I always put the checks on top," he said. "Tomorrow is *Reader's Digest* day, and then *Modern Maturity*. I can almost tell you what day it is by what's in the mail."

"At least you feel that way because it's your job," said Mary Ellen. "Imagine if you could do that because it's all you live for. You do have a life other than your job, don't you? How are things goin' between you and that Wentworth girl?"

Austin bristled slightly at Mary Ellen's direct prying. She was a good supervisor, but she had no social graces.

"We've enjoyed several activities together," said Austin.

"Whoa!" said Mary Ellen, grinning.

"Mostly at her mother's home," said Austin. "As a matter of fact, we're going to be together this evening at my father's house, planting some bulbs."

"How romantic," said Mary Ellen, rolling her eyes upward and shaking her head. "Why don't you take the girl to dinner and a movie? How about a concert?"

Austin, who disliked talking about his personal life at work, turned and stared at her. "Because she prefers to do things at home," he said evenly in his most controlled and well-modulated voice. "She's a very home-loving person. Now I'm going to work."

"Touchy, touchy," Mary Ellen said to Libby, another carrier, as Austin drove away. "That Jocelyn is a cutie. Can't imagine what she sees in a stiff like Austin."

"Then you're blind as well as dim-witted," remarked Libby. "He's a hunk, and financially, he's set. Who wouldn't be interested?"

"Me," said Mary Ellen. "I don't think I'd like dating a corpse."

Austin would never have admitted to Mary Ellen or Libby how much he looked forward to delivering Social Security checks. Mrs. Duimstra would undoubtedly meet him with a foam cup of hot tea and a slice of banana bread. She lived in an old ranch house built during the postwar boom. It now sat on the edge of the road surrounded by new half-million dollar homes on what used to be the Duimstra family's apple orchard.

Austin had learned about her through conversations and through the mail delivered to her home. There were regular bank statements, thick envelopes from investment firms and law offices, and lots of registered letters from real estate agents. He figured she really didn't need the Social Security check.

By now, Austin knew who was at home during the day, where the big dogs were, who had the most credit cards, who shopped by mail, and where and when most families went on vacation. He knew details about each customer and felt responsible for each and every one.

As he came to the house where he had seen the boy and

girl playing in the yard, Austin reached for the large package addressed to Gerald Folkert. It was from a photography supply company. He was surprised to see a man walking toward the road. As Austin stopped at the box, the man hailed him.

"Got a package for me?" he asked. He was tall and lanky, with a thick, dark mustache. His dark brown hair curled over the edge of his collar and drooped over his pale forehead. He had the look of a cowboy just recovered from an illness, an effect enhanced by his faded, low-slung jeans and scuffed, stacked-heel boots.

Austin nodded and handed him the box. "Photographer? I'm an amateur myself, but I see you do business with a professional company."

Gerald Folkert took the parcel. "I make a living at it, but you won't find my stuff in galleries," he said.

"My name's Austin Van Doran. I see your children have something better to do today than make faces at me."

Gerald looked at him blankly for a moment, and frowned slightly. Then he said, "Yes, it's a school day."

"If you don't mind my asking, is that bulk film? I've been wondering if I could save any money loading my own film just for the hobby work I do."

Gerald shrugged. "Maybe, if you use enough of it. You have to make sure you don't keep it too long, though." They talked prices and brands for a moment, then Austin pulled away and headed on toward Jocelyn's home.

"I just met another one of your neighbors," said Austin, when he found Jocelyn waiting at the mailbox. "Gerald Folkert, the man with the house up on the hill."

Jocelyn looked at him warily. "Did you like him?"

"Of course," said Austin. "He's a photographer. I enjoy photography myself."

Jocelyn gave him a sideways look. "Well, he wanted to take my picture and I refused. I think he's kind of creepy."

"What's wrong with wanting to take your picture? I think he has a portrait studio in his home. He probably just wanted your photo for his portfolio."

"Maybe. No registered mail today?"

Austin sensed a note of weariness in her voice. He shook his head. "What's wrong?"

She smiled fleetingly and lifted her shoulders, her arms filled with mail. "Nothing."

Suddenly, Austin thought of Mary Ellen's remarks.

"You seem depressed. Let me take you out for a nice evening. It's such a beautiful day. We can still get an outdoor table at the Inn. Look, the leaves are already getting some color. Come on, it will cheer you up. You don't have to dress up. I'll go in jeans, too."

"That's sweet," said Jocelyn, "but you look like you just came from a trunk show no matter what you're wearing. I can't believe I'm hearing you try to cheer me up." Her voice was regaining its normal lilt, and the sparkle was coming back to her face. "I'm fine, really. I just have a lot of work to do." She quickly glanced through the top layer of envelopes and suddenly her face lit up. She put everything down on the shoulder of the road and opened one of the letters.

"Austin, I've won some money! Celebrate with me. I'll cook dinner."

Austin remembered Jocelyn's house, and hesitated.

"Well, all right," he said. "If you won't let me take you out,

I'll come over. Congratulations. Does this happen often?"

"Huh!" she said. "I collect plenty of times, *plenty of times!* How else could I maintain this lavish lifestyle?" She waved as Austin pulled away, then went inside to finish going through the mail. After a while, she put on her sneakers and began walking east on Greenwood. She knew today was Greta's day off.

"Hi-ya!" Greta sang when she saw Jocelyn. "Whatcha doing? Did you come to see me, or are you just walking for your health?" Greta lived in a small brick house that belonged to her parents, who had recently moved to Florida. Over her polyester retro-style outfit, she wore the pink smock that was her work uniform at the walk-in salon where she was a stylist.

"Hi, Greta," said Jocelyn. "I came to see you. Austin's coming to my house for dinner tonight. Got any good ideas on what I should fix?"

Greta's expression changed to one of excited surprise. "Forget what you're going to cook, silly. Think about what you're going to wear." She clasped her hands beneath her chin. "Please, *please* let me do your hair!"

Jocelyn came into the house and sat down at the dining room table where Greta's vast collection of cosmetics was piled. She had nail polish in twenty shades with lipstick to match, and a full palette of liquid foundation and eye colors. There were lip and eyeliner pencils, brushes, sponges, and cotton pads strewn on the table. When Greta sat down, however, her reach was sure and true as she picked up the nail polish remover, an orange stick, and a cotton swab and began working on her nails as she talked to Jocelyn.

"You're kidding," she said. "Austin invited you to the Inn, and you said no? It's a great place, and so romantic. I thought you liked him."

"I do," replied Jocelyn, "but I can't go out with him anywhere except to our parent's homes or my place. Greta, look at me," said Jocelyn.

Greta looked up at her friend. "So? I'm looking."

Jocelyn laced her fingers through her hair. "My hair's a wreck. I've been cutting it myself for the last six months. I don't have a drop of makeup left. Most of all, I don't have a thing to wear."

"Then let's go shopping," suggested Greta. "All the new fall things are in the stores now. I'll drive. I wouldn't want to be seen in your car."

"Greta, I couldn't drive my car anyway. The insurance has lapsed and I can't afford to renew it. I can't afford to put gas in it. Don't you understand? I have no money."

"I thought you were into this contest thing, and it was paying off for you."

"Don't tell anyone. I don't want my mother to know, but I'm making just enough to keep alive. I can't buy any clothes. I sold everything I had just to keep going last spring when I moved into Aunt Bebe's place."

"Well, don't be so proud," said Greta. "Ask your mom for a loan. Ask *me* for a loan."

Jocelyn's expression was hard. "No! I appreciate your generosity, but I won't go into debt, especially not to my mother. And I won't borrow from you when I don't know if I could pay it back. I'll just have to make do with what I have, and if Austin doesn't like me in my present wardrobe, well, too bad."

"Come on," said Greta. "Let's go down to your place and look at what you've got. Maybe I can come up with a new approach, some new combination that will look a bit more elegant than that sweatshirt."

"Well, I don't know. There isn't much to work with."

"Oh, come on, it will be fun. Trust me, I'm a genius when it comes to accessorizing," said Greta, replacing the cap on her polish remover and grabbing her purse. Together they got into her car and drove to Jocelyn's home a mile away.

Greta stood in front of the closet and laughed. "Are you serious? Is this it?"

"That's it, except for what I have on."

"That hardly counts," said Greta, looking at Jocelyn's worn sweatshirt and ragged sweatpants. She turned back to the closet and shook her head. There was a threadbare red plaid flannel shirt, and a blue one in a larger size in better shape. A long-sleeved sweatshirt was folded on the shelf above the clothes bar. Next to it was Jocelyn's "good" sweat suit, which she wore to the grocery store or other public places. Her sandals rested on the closet floor. Her athletic shoes, purchased at a garage sale early in the summer, were on her feet. One pair of jeans hung on a hanger. Another was draped over the back of a chair.

"If only you and I were the same size," said Greta, whose long legs and torso sent her towering over Jocelyn by nearly eight inches. "Then I could loan you something."

"Never mind," Jocelyn said, nearly out of patience with the whole exercise. "I don't care much about clothes anyway. That's why I sold my things last spring. I just didn't think about dating. How did I know someone like Austin would come along?"

"I'm beginning to see something here," began Greta, ignoring her friend. "I'm thinking eclectic styling, the orphaned waif, country comes to town. It could be the perfect look for you. You do have underwear, don't you?"

"Well, yes," laughed Jocelyn. "Nobody would have bought that."

"All right, I know what we'll do. You'll be stunning in your own unique way when I get through with you." She stood back-to-back with Jocelyn, then said, "You're short, but you're wider than me. You can borrow a top. I've got just the thing. Now, what about dinner? You said you won some money. What are you going to cook?"

"I really didn't win much. I just wanted Austin to think it was a lot so he'd be happy and not worry about me. I think he's beginning to catch on. I mean, at first, I think he just thought I was eccentric."

"Now why would he think that?" Greta quipped.

"I mean, like my car. I let him think it was a collector's item, and I was keeping it in hopes of increasing my investment. It's really just an old car. I'll never have the thousands of dollars it would take to restore it. If I had the money, I'd buy a good car. I think he's figured that out."

"Well, time for all that when you two are alone," said Greta. "You can't go wrong with a couple of steaks for dinner. Have you got a grill?"

Jocelyn nodded. "Somewhere, I think, in the shed out back."

"Get it going, and let Austin cook the meat. You fix a salad and bake a couple of potatoes. You can feed both of you for about ten bucks. How much did you win?"

"Twenty-five dollars," Jocelyn said, "but I have to pay a light bill or I'll be without electricity by the end of the week."

"All right, get cheap steaks and marinate them," suggested Greta. "Now let's go back to my house and get busy creating the kind of feminine allure Austin won't be able to resist. I'll run you to the store first."

Jocelyn grabbed Greta in an affectionate squeeze. "You're a peach, Greta. I've said it before, and I'll say it again. A peach!"

As they left the house, Greta asked, "Are you sure you don't want to use my lawn mower and cut the grass? Austin sounds like the kind of guy who likes things neat."

Jocelyn shrugged. "It hasn't been cut all summer. Why should I start now? Maybe some farmer will offer to buy it as hay."

ð

When Austin arrived, he smelled the hot charcoal and saw a thin stream of smoke rising from behind the house, and was reassured. He half-expected to find that Jocelyn had forgotten about dinner, or had changed her mind. The funny thing was, he was getting used to her whims and unpredictability. He was beginning to enjoy the surprises. It was the example of her warmth and spontaneity, he realized, that had helped him open up to the customers on his route, to begin thinking of them as friends instead of house numbers.

He went to the back of the house, kicking his way through the knee-high grass that was now gone to seed and beginning to turn brown. The grill had to be nearby. There was smoke in the air, but the smell was no longer charcoal. As he rounded the far corner of the house, he saw flames licking at the flaking paint on the side of the house. A room-sized portion of the yard around the grill was on fire.

"Jocelyn!" he yelled in the direction of the back door. "Call the fire department!"

He looked for a hose, but found only an outside faucet. "Jocelyn!" he shouted again. He could not wait for her. When he turned on the faucet, a thin stream of orange-brown water trickled for a moment, then stopped. It was not connected to the main water supply. Austin ran back to his car, got a fire extinguisher, and began attacking the flames.

Jocelyn came out the side door, saw what had happened, and ran back inside. In a moment she had returned with two pitchers of water. She tossed them onto the fire, then ran back for more.

"Call the fire department!" Austin shouted again when she returned.

"Can't!" she yelled. "No phone!"

Austin worked from the edges of the fire toward the grill in the center, starting with the side nearest the house. Jocelyn threw the water in a wide pattern, dampening as much as possible. In only a few minutes the fire was out, but Austin was livid.

"How could you start a fire in the middle of this hay field and go off and leave it?" he demanded. "The grass is as high as the grill! You could have lost your house. Never walk away from a grill. Bring all your food outside before you start the fire, then stay and watch it. And get a phone! You can't live alone without a telephone."

"I can and I do," said Jocelyn, struggling to control her own trembling, but refusing to be cowed by his outburst. "I can take care of myself just fine!"

They faced off for a few seconds, then Jocelyn jokingly said, "Too bad we didn't have any marshmallows."

Austin suddenly pulled her close, smelling the smoke in her hair and knowing his anger was a thin veil for his fear. "Don't you ever think about the consequences?" he murmured. "Is everything just one adventure after another for you?"

"I can't breathe," she mumbled, her face pressed flat against his chest. He let her go, but for a moment she stayed close, savoring the comfort of another human being who cared and was concerned. When she lifted her face, she was an inch away from the edge of his beard. *That beard just has to go,* she thought.

Jocelyn stepped back, and for the first time Austin noticed what she was wearing. Jocelyn had borrowed from Greta a silky, bright blue shell, and over it she wore the oversized blue plaid flannel shirt, buttons open halfway down, sleeves rolled almost to her elbows, and the shirttails knotted at her waist. She wore her best jeans, ironed smooth, and on her feet were Greta's blue leather mules, a facial tissue stuffed into the toe of each one to fill the extra space. She also had borrowed a pair of large clustered rhinestone earrings and a matching pendant.

"Is your sweatshirt at the cleaners?" asked Austin as they walked to the car to put away the fire extinguisher.

"Greta helped me design the outfit."

"Greta DeGroot, 108 Greenwood?" Jocelyn nodded, and Austin said, "Remind me to deliver a thank-you card to her."

"Do you like it?" Jocelyn turned in front of him like a schoolgirl hoping for a compliment. Austin was caught up in the color and glitter and in her brilliant smile. It was the first time he had seen her wearing makeup and Greta's talents had not been wasted. Every good feature Jocelyn had was accented by light and color and shadow.

"You do look stunning," he said quietly.

"Greta said I would," said Jocelyn. "She's a peach. I already told her that. I'm really hungry now. I hope that grill's still hot. I got steaks. Do you want to cook them?"

"By all means."

Jocelyn had set the table with quilted place mats, and there were wildflowers in a glass tumbler in the center. Two small, scented votive candles burned on either side of the centerpiece. Austin had to admit there was a certain charm about the meal, but if there had been no meal, it wouldn't have mattered. He could not take his eyes off Jocelyn.

Her hair, which Greta had pinned up in back and curled around her face, had come a bit loose while she fought the fire. A few strands hung along her neck and over one ear. Her face, with its accented features, glowed in the candlelight, and when she moved, the earrings caught the colors and made it seem as if she were an island maiden with flowers fastened in her hair.

After a second cup of the fine coffee, Austin reached across the table and covered her hand with his.

"Jocelyn, you must be more careful," he said. "What if I hadn't been here?"

"If you hadn't been here," she admitted, "I would not have been grilling steaks."

He leaned back in the chair, exasperated. "Oh, all right,

make a joke of it. You know it's dangerous to be here all
by yourself with no telephone."

"It's very peaceful," she said.

"Well, now that you have some money coming in, I hope
you'll think about safety. You need a smoke detector, and a
fire extinguisher, and yes, a telephone."

They took their coffee cups and went to the living room as
the sun was slipping below the tree line. Jocelyn took a pile
of papers from on top of the shade and turned on a lamp.

"Doesn't this ever bother you?" asked Austin, looking
around at the accumulation.

"What?"

"Everything lying around like this. It's so—messy."

She looked at him a moment, not sure whether she
should be offended. "Messy? I don't think so. Messy is
when you just let things fall, and don't have any plan. I
know where everything is. This is how I want it. It's a
friendly house. Everything is close to me."

"I'll have to agree with you on that," said Austin. Jocelyn
had not yet visited his home. He had assumed she would
love the neat, ordered, open space, the tasteful furniture carefully arrayed according to a professional decorating plan.
Not until this moment had he considered that she might not
like his house, might even consider it inferior to her own. No
one had ever called his place "friendly." Though his guests
(could he call them friends?) often complimented him on
the house, they never dropped in just to say hello.

They watched the sunset fade to darkness and talked
about their work. Hardly realizing it, Austin held Jocelyn's
hand as he sat beside her, gently rubbing his thumb on the
short, smooth, polished nails, more of Greta's handiwork.

"When I finished my training as a dental assistant, I got a job right away," explained Jocelyn. "There's a big demand for that kind of work. I could still be doing it today, but I hated it. I hated wearing the uniform, and I hated the smell of the place. I hated spending all day with people who couldn't talk to me because their mouths were propped open. I hated causing people discomfort, even if it was for their own good."

"Why did you ever choose that field?" Austin asked. "You said you graduated at sixteen. You must have academic ability. Why didn't you go to college, learn something different?"

Jocelyn shrugged. "I wanted to do something right away. I wanted to be on my own, and it was work I could do without spending years and years in school. I thought I would like it, but people don't usually like dental workers much. I want to be liked, don't you?"

Austin smiled. He did, but popularity had never been one of his career considerations. "But, contests! Why contests?"

"I read a newspaper article about someone right here in town who is a professional contestant. I knew there wasn't much money in it to begin with, but it also costs nothing to get started. When Aunt Bebe died and left me this house, I knew I wanted to come here to live and have a business of my own of some kind. It was either contests or selling something, and I decided to try contests. I love it, Austin! It's the most fun."

"Don't you ever think about—well, you know, whether it's right? I mean, people must think. . ." His voice trailed off, and he found himself staring at the floor.

"I've never much cared what people think, but I know

what you're talking about," Jocelyn said. "You think I'm a gambler, don't you?"

"Well, what's the difference? Sweepstakes, the lottery—it's all something for nothing."

Jocelyn answered patiently, "It isn't all the same, Austin. I work hard every day. The contests I enter are promotional advertising. They are pushing a product. I'm helping them by participating. Lots of times I write things, like slogans or jingles, that I know the company uses for its own benefit. When I win money or products, I'm just getting paid for services. It isn't like betting on a horse race, where it's strictly chance and the hope of getting something for nothing. I *don't* gamble," she said emphatically. "I never risk anything, except the price of the postage, and that's just an expense any business owner would have."

Austin realized she had carefully thought through her own ethics, and there was a certain wisdom in her choice. She had started a business of her own with no greater investment than a roll of stamps, and she worked hard every day. It was certainly as good a life for her as standing behind a cash register or packing parts off an assembly line.

"If you're happy, I'm happy," he said. "I will say I'm glad you won that coffeemaker. I'm going to get another cup, if you don't mind."

He stepped around the items in the hall on his way to the kitchen and poured another cup of coffee. He decided it might be good with a little milk, and opened the refrigerator door. There was nothing inside.

Austin stood staring at the bare shelves, the light shining starkly on the white interior. There was no milk. There were no eggs, no cheese, no meat. In the door were a few packets of mustard from a fast-food restaurant, and on the bottom shelf was half a head of lettuce, which Austin guessed was left over from their supper.

He closed the door and opened the old-fashioned pantry. Though the walls were lined with shelves, they were almost completely bare. There were a few cans of soup, two five-pound bags of flour, and five large boxes filled with bottles of ketchup. Austin figured they were another of Jocelyn's contest prizes.

Quietly, he began looking through the kitchen cupboards. There was one half-empty box of dry cereal, a few spices, a cake mix, and an eight-ounce jar of peanut butter next to half a loaf of white bread. That was all. Austin realized that despite her brave talk, Jocelyn was making next to nothing in her business, and probably had since the beginning.

He took his coffee and returned to the living room. What should he say? He was overwhelmed with a desire to confront her, persuade her to take a loan from him, or to encourage her to find a job. He wondered about the amount of the check he had delivered today. Was it enough for her to live on for a week? A day? How much had she spent on their evening?

"You worry a lot, don't you?" Jocelyn asked after a few moments of silence. "I don't worry much. Things always seem to turn out all right, one way or another. Look at us, for instance. I wasn't even—" she stopped abruptly and jumped up from the couch.

"You weren't what?" Austin asked, but she was busy closing the mismatched curtains against the night.

"Let's go outside," she said. "It's wonderful this time of year."

They took the two kitchen chairs out to the front porch and listened to the night sounds emanating from the wetlands around the house.

"I had been here for just about two weeks last spring," Jocelyn reminisced, "and there was a real warm day. I went outside in the evening, and there was this chorus of frogs and peepers that just burst from the swamp. I'd never heard anything like it. That's what happens when you grow up in the suburbs. We need to leave some wild places so things like that can happen."

"I agree with you in the abstract," Austin said, slapping a mosquito, "but I like things to be manageable. I guess the wild places are fine. Right up there is a good example of preservation." He nodded in the direction of the nearby botanical gardens, marked by a faint glow in the sky. "Personally I like to visit the wild places, but I wouldn't want to live there."

"Good!" said Jocelyn. "If you go there to live, they won't be wild anymore."

Austin thought of Mrs. Duimstra. "You know, this place could be very valuable. It's the best of both worlds, just what most people want. You're close to the city, but out in the country. How much property do you have?"

"I think about five acres," she said. "There's an old orchard back there, and deer come up and feed on the windfalls."

Obviously she has no idea what five acres of land on this road could be worth, Austin thought. A developer could turn it into ten or twenty homes. She was sitting on a gold mine, and living on ketchup sandwiches.

Reluctantly, he said, "I have to go home. I get up early."

"How early?"

"About 4:30. They tell me when the snow starts, I'll have to start even earlier than that."

She nodded. "I get up at 5:00. I can't sleep later than that."

Austin did not rise to leave. There was nothing more to say, but he did not want to go. *This is how it should be,* he thought.

Jocelyn took in the beauty of the night, happy just to be with him. *This is how it should be,* she thought.

A car passed slowly, the driver apparently looking for house numbers. Austin and Jocelyn watched as it went down the road, slowing, stopping, then backing up to turn in at Gerald Folkert's house.

"Who would be visiting that guy?" Jocelyn muttered.

"He seems perfectly nice to me, though his children are a bit rude."

Jocelyn frowned. "He doesn't have any children."

"They were at his house when school started," Austin said.

"Well, if he ever had any children, he probably ate them."

"Jocelyn!"

She laughed. "He's just creepy! I don't mind if you like him. I don't. Go home, Austin. I don't want to read in the paper that you fell asleep at the wheel and drove into the river and know it's my fault."

He took her hand as they stood up to walk to the car. "If I did, would you be sad?"

"Of course. What a question."

"Jocelyn," he began, "I never expected to. . .well, I had

a certain kind of person in mind, you know, for. . ."

"Shush," she murmured, gently placing a finger against his lips. "That's the kind of talk that's best reserved for letters."

four

November

When Jocelyn awakened, the room was pitch dark, but she knew it was morning. She sat up on the old-fashioned wire-spring bed, put her bare feet over the side, but then hesitated. She knew how cold the hardwood floor would be. For a moment she sat there, feet dangling, adjusting to the cold air.

My grace is sufficient for you, for my power is made perfect in weakness.

Though she could not read the words in the predawn darkness, Jocelyn knew they were there, hanging on the wall above the metal frame bed, another cross-stitched sampler left behind by Aunt Bebe. She pulled the cheap comforter up around her shoulders and wondered why a strong woman like her great-aunt would think such a Bible verse was inspiring or comforting. This fascination with the Bible was the one aspect of Aunt Bebe that was a mystery to Jocelyn.

Suddenly, she jumped from the bed and scampered to the bathroom, taking care not to slip on the bath towel that was passing for a rug on the cold tile bathroom floor. She turned on the water and let it run until steam clouded the mirror and enveloped the chilly room.

Next to the bathroom mirror was another verse: *When I*

57

am weak, then I am strong.

Except for the Bible reference stitched beneath the words, the enigmatic phrase could be a Chinese proverb, Jocelyn thought as she washed her face and combed her hair. But Aunt Bebe had believed the Bible had a special quality above and beyond the wisdom literature of other cultures.

She had been weak, Jocelyn remembered, wasting away in a nursing home, humbled by cancer, but uncomplaining. Still, as Jocelyn pulled the comforter together under her chin with one hand and brushed her teeth with the other, she knew Aunt Bebe had an inner strength. She knew who she was. She never questioned the direction of her life. It was the quality Jocelyn most loved about her. *Did Aunt Bebe stitch those verses before or after she received the doctor's diagnosis?* Jocelyn wondered.

Warmed a bit from the steamy bathroom air, she dressed in jeans and flannel shirt, thick socks, and an old pair of men's slippers she had found at a thrift store. They were warmer than her sneakers. Soon, she decided, she would have to do something about getting some oil for the furnace. During the spring and summer, the sun had warmed the house enough to keep it livable, but winter was just around the corner.

As usual, Jocelyn worked at the kitchen table, huddled over a cup of coffee. Checks had been coming in at a rate of one or two a week, but never in large amounts. It confirmed to Jocelyn that her research into the contest industry had been accurate; the bread and butter was in the smaller prizes, but the gravy was in the large ones. So far she had only bread, and not much of that, but she was alive. Her mother had stopped dropping in with food that she tried to pass off as leftovers, and had apparently accepted Jocelyn's new career.

Jocelyn worked until mid-morning when it was time for Austin to arrive. She made half a pot of coffee, noting that only a dozen or so packets of the rich blend remained. When she saw the white truck coming down the road, she poured a cup of coffee and walked out to meet him.

As she approached, Austin smiled at the memory of their summer encounter. How long ago it seemed! The days had passed, fall was nearly gone, and he had spent so little time with her. He took the coffee cup she held out to him, and he thought how she had changed in the past weeks. Then as he sipped the steaming, aromatic liquid, he wondered if it was she who had changed, or his perception of her.

Last week he had come to her house in the evening after a heavy windstorm to make sure her roof was undamaged, and that none of the many trees around the house had fallen across power lines. He found her balancing her checkbook by candlelight.

"What's all this?" he asked, pointing to several large envelopes stuffed with paper.

"Check stubs, receipts for stamps, things like that," she answered.

He began sorting through the papers, trying to appear casual. "Are you filing quarterly payments for income tax?"

She shook her head. "I haven't even thought about taxes. I'll worry about it at the end of the year," she said. "I've saved everything, all my check stubs."

"Have you been putting money aside to pay taxes?" he asked.

"I probably won't have to pay," she said. "I don't think I'll actually make any profit."

"But you will," said Austin. "Even though you don't think you have any money, if you earned anything at all, it's income. And what about the cash value of things like your coffeemaker, and that ketchup in the pantry? Since this is your first year in business, you aren't necessarily expected to show a profit, but you still might have to pay."

Jocelyn frowned. "Really? I thought I might get a return."

"Have you paid any taxes yet?" Austin persisted.

When Jocelyn shook her head, Austin continued. "You only get a return if you pay in more than you owe. The government doesn't give cash bonuses for doing a good job."

"I just haven't thought much about it," she said with a flutter of her hand, as if she was chasing away a troublesome insect.

"I'll help you," he offered. "Don't throw anything away. At the end of the year I'll help you file your return."

Jocelyn looked at him, a slight smile on her face. "How you do go on. You just can't believe I could do this alone, do you? Do I seem that stupid?"

"No! No, Jocelyn, I didn't mean to imply that at all," he said. "But—" he could not say he was worried about her, because he knew it would only confirm her suspicions that he considered her inept. Helping was the only thing he knew, the only thing he did well. Meeting needs was his one sure way to relate to people, but she did not need him. In fact, he could not exactly define why he wanted so much to be part of her life. Did he need her more than she needed him?

"Don't even think about it," she said, patting his arm as though she were his grandmother. "It's a nice thought, and I appreciate it. But it will work out."

Now, as Austin sat in his mail truck savoring the last few sips of coffee, Jocelyn shoveled her mail into shopping bags.

"I talked to my mother yesterday," said Jocelyn. "She's invited both of us for Thanksgiving dinner. Would you like to come? I promise not to push you into the gravy."

For Austin, there was no question. He loved spending time with Jocelyn. He also loved spending time with Adelle. It seemed to him they had all settled into a kind of comfortable, friendly companionship. He wondered where it would lead. *Probably nowhere,* he thought, *as long as it's a threesome, but for now it's all right.*

"I'd love to spend the day with you and Adelle," Austin said. "My father will be out of town on a sales trip." He did not mention that he rarely spent holidays with his father and that he had not had a real Thanksgiving since his parents' divorce.

"Will you call Mother and tell her we'll be there?" Jocelyn asked. "If you'll come and get me, I'd appreciate it." She had purchased minimal insurance and could now legally drive the car, but the tires were bad and the engine undependable. She used the vehicle only for necessary short trips. Besides, she thought her mother was embarrassed to have the car in her driveway.

Jocelyn took the empty cup from Austin's hand and tucked it into one of her bags.

"Do you really take care of all your mail the same day you receive it?" Austin asked.

Jocelyn nodded. "Within twenty-four hours. Sometimes I have to work late."

He offered a searching look, and Jocelyn sighed. "All right! Yes, I'm making a little more money these days, partly because I've just continued to enter for a longer period of time. But overall, my personal income is up nearly 10 percent from last summer. Can you say the same?"

"No, but I didn't start at zero," Austin said. "Just remember you can depend on me if you need anything."

How well she knew! It was one of the qualities that had immediately drawn her to Austin, but had also rankled her on several occasions. It wasn't that she didn't want Austin's help. She just didn't want to feel like a project. She was afraid that if she accepted his help in the form of a loan or even to repair her car or work in the house, he would forever see her as a teacher sees a student—almost like a father sees a daughter. They had become friends over the past months, but Jocelyn wanted more than friendship. She was beginning to wonder whether Austin had more than that to offer.

As he pulled away, she remembered the first day she had met him, and recalled the excitement and sense of expectation he had aroused in her. Was it all just childish infatuation? He had yet to say he loved her, or even that he liked her.

She waved good-bye and went back to the house to tackle a new stack of mail and enter a few more contests. The money was not important. She had learned that from Aunt Bebe, who obviously had not accumulated a fortune, based on the house and the furnishings she had left behind. What mattered was the satisfaction, the independence, and the enjoyment of doing something you could do well. And Jocelyn did love what she was doing. Each day seemed like Christmas to her.

Inside, she dumped the bags on the floor, got down on her knees and began sorting, always with an eye to the personal letter that could mean a check. "Come on, come on," she murmured, her fingers flying. "Just a little one to pay for some fuel oil so I don't freeze this winter," she was saying. "I need tires. I need milk. I need stamps."

Suddenly, she realized that she was actually praying. She certainly was not talking to herself, and she had the distinct impression that someone was listening. She paused, resting her weight on both hands.

Cast all your anxiety on him because he cares for you, was Aunt Bebe's living room verse. It was done in large gold letters with green ivy twining around an oversized *C*. Jocelyn looked up at it, then sat cross-legged on the floor.

"If You are listening, God, You know I am not complaining," Jocelyn whispered in the direction of the plaque. "I'm only asking for what I earn. If You control all things, then You control these contests. Please. Send me some money."

She went back to work and found many, many opportunities for entries, but not a single check. When she got up from the floor, she stretched her tired limbs, pivoted her head to loosen her stiff neck, and stepped closer to the wall directly in front of the Bible verse. *What did Aunt Bebe know that I don't know?* she wondered.

&

Thanksgiving Day was typically colorless. The trees, except for the oaks, were bare and the leaves on the ground ruined by the recent cold rains. Still, there was a sensual satisfaction in the bleakness of it all, the spent look of the landscape, the smoldering colors completely without heat, but not without life. Austin looked at the bare woods and felt the threat of winter as he drove down Greenwood Road, Jocelyn in the car beside him. Could this actually be a holiday?

The sunless afternoon made Jocelyn's house look like an abandoned shell as Austin watched it diminish behind him in the side mirror. He found himself scheming to get Jocelyn to live somewhere else, and it occurred to him that he could ask her to marry him. That would solve her problems, but what about his own?

Austin lately had begun to notice that all the things he had wanted in life had come to him. The attractive home and the solid, secure job were things he could look to with pride and say he had planned them and made them happen. *Why,* he wondered, *is it all so disappointing?* Was he clamoring to rescue Jocelyn because the other accomplishments in his life had failed to satisfy him and he now needed a new goal to pursue? Marriage! It was something to think about.

When they arrived at Adelle Wentworth's home, the aroma of roasted turkey greeted them. Adelle took Austin's overcoat and Jocelyn's outdated nylon parka with equal grace, but Austin caught a glimpse of her checking the frayed cuffs of Jocelyn's jacket, and noted her troubled expression. He knew it was hard for her to be shut out of her daughter's life; and as always, he wondered what had come between them.

Adelle had built a small fire in the living room fireplace, and she and Austin sat near it and chatted while Jocelyn flitted about the house, looking for books she wanted to borrow, checking through the mail her mother had saved for her examination, and asking questions about relatives. After a few minutes, she wandered into the living room.

"How long until dinner?" Jocelyn asked.

Adelle answered, "It will be about an hour. Have some trail mix." She held out the bowl of nuts, candy, and raisins to Jocelyn, who ate some, then took a handful and passed the bowl to Austin. "I was just wondering," she said. "You don't have flowers on the table. You always have flowers."

"When I went to the florist's shop yesterday, it was closed," Adelle replied. "I didn't have time to go elsewhere. We'll have to make do with candles."

"I'll fix something," said Jocelyn. She grabbed her jacket and went outside.

"Austin, please feel free to go along," said Adelle. "I've a few things left to do in the kitchen anyway."

"I'll help you," offered Austin, rising from the sofa. "I'm a little slow on the uptake sometimes, but I think I'm beginning to understand that Jocelyn doesn't want my help."

"Or anyone else's," said Adelle as they went into the kitchen. "If she were one degree less charming, she'd be a real pain. I love her, though. I know she thinks I disapprove of her, but I am very proud of the way she has lived since high school."

Austin chopped apples for a Waldorf salad, and ventured a question. "Why do you think there seems to be such friction between you?"

Adelle offered a sad smile. "I know perfectly well," she said. "Jocelyn was a daddy's girl, and felt he could do no wrong. When she was about eight, he left home for a few months. We didn't tell her then because she was so young, but we were having problems. We had decided to separate. It might have been permanent, but we received good counseling, and we also discovered a new spiritual dimension that helped us overcome our problems. Jocelyn only knew her daddy was gone. When he came home, she clung to him all the more, shutting me out."

Austin listened without looking, busy with the salad. Adelle seemed to recite the story without emotion, but perhaps it was just her high degree of control.

"My husband was a good provider. He was a highly successful industrial chemical sales representative. Not only was he talented, he worked extremely hard. When he died—he had a sudden heart attack while driving and was killed when his car hit an abutment—Jocelyn was devastated. For a while, I feared she might not recover. Then she translated her pain into anger directed at me, a childish device, but powerful. It was like the first time he had been gone, but even more calculating and severe."

"Adelle, this is quite personal. Don't feel you have to—"

"You might as well know," said Adelle. "I doubt that Jocelyn will ever tell you her feelings. I doubt she even knows her feelings. Gradually, she convinced herself that her father had worked himself to death trying to give me all the things I wanted. She once said that if he had not been trying to buy—" she took a deep breath and slowly exhaled, then continued, "to buy back my love and forgiveness, that he would still be alive." Adelle put down the paring knife and put both hands briefly to her face.

"She doesn't know that you and your husband had reconciled?"

"She has heard the words, but only from me, after my husband died. She has no faith or trust in me anymore. I know of nothing I can do to win it back."

Jocelyn came in through the kitchen door, carrying a paper sack filled with leaves, acorns, twigs, dead weeds, some bird feathers, and a moss-covered stone about the size of an egg. Whistling softly, she looked into a couple of cupboards until she found a wooden dish shaped like a palm leaf with the edges curled up. She got a sheet of newspaper, crumpled it tightly, placed it in the dish, and used it for the base of the centerpiece she envisioned.

Austin watched her, amazed at her creativity. His first thought was that she could make money doing such work, but he knew better than to say anything about it. Not only did Jocelyn not want his help, she did not want his advice.

"Too bad your father isn't in town," said Jocelyn to Austin. "We could have invited him. Austin's father invents games," she said to her mother. "He doesn't live far from me."

"What's your father's name?" asked Adelle.

"Martin Van Doran. He's on a business trip, looking for a buyer for his new game. He's hoping to get in on the Christmas market for next year."

Adelle scowled slightly. "Martin Van Doran. Is your mother's name Sylvia?"

"Yes. She doesn't live with him anymore. They divorced when I was in high school."

"I'm sorry," said Adelle. "I think my husband and I worked with Martin and Sylvia Van Doran at the downtown summer festival one year. We volunteered to cook at a church food booth. We made steak sandwiches."

Austin nodded. "That would have been when they were

attending that big church on the highway. We all started going there about the time I was in junior high. I think they were looking for something that would heal their marriage. It didn't work."

"I can't say I knew them well," Adelle said. "We were attending church there on a somewhat irregular basis ourselves. I only knew your parents through that volunteer work."

"When Dad gets back into town, we'll do something together," suggested Austin.

Adelle pulled the turkey from the oven, and put the wild rice pilaf in to warm while she cooked vegetables and got cold dishes from the refrigerator.

Jocelyn placed her centerpiece on the table and it was perfect, the rich earthen colors in soft contrast to the creamy ivory candlesticks and tapers her mother had placed on the unbleached lace tablecloth.

"What a lovely meal," Austin said as they sat down. "This is the nicest Thanksgiving Day I can remember." He looked at Jocelyn, and wondered what she was thinking.

"Dad always used to pray," she said quietly, focusing on the candles, and Austin realized that even now, her pain was like a stone slung around her neck.

"Austin, would you like to give thanks?" asked Adelle.

Austin knew the Christian origins of Thanksgiving, and he was conscious of a higher power directing history. But speaking words to that higher power was not his habit. Still, he did not want to offend. He bowed his head.

"Oh God, Maker of heaven and earth," he began, trying to focus his thoughts, "You have provided all good things for us. Thank You for this meal. We eat together today to remember all the goodness of nature. Thank You for this food, and for our friendship. Amen."

Austin concentrated on his plate as Adelle began serving, not sure how the prayer would be received. *Was it a prayer?* he wondered. Had he been speaking to Adelle and Jocelyn, or to that higher power? Was there anyone out there listening? As he sampled the stuffing and sweet potatoes, he thought about the similarity between Jocelyn's parents and his own. Both had sought solace and healing in the church when their marriages faltered. According to Adelle, her marriage had been healed, but her relationship with her daughter remained broken. His parents' marriage had failed, and he knew conflicts remained between himself and his father. He only wished he could verbalize them as well as Adelle Wentworth did her own.

After a game of Scrabble, which Adelle easily won, they watched the final quarter of a football game and had pie and coffee. Austin was so comfortable he wished he might never leave, but he sensed Jocelyn's restlessness.

"What do you have planned for the evening?" asked Adelle.

"I've got a ton of work," said Jocelyn. "For government workers, it's a holiday, but not for me." Quickly she put her hand across her mouth, then turned to Austin. "No offense," she said.

He laughed. "None taken," he replied, and rose to go. "I'm going in early tomorrow, anyway. The official beginning of the Christmas rush, you know."

Austin was surprised to receive a brief hug from Adelle, and to see her also embrace Jocelyn as they went to the door.

"It's been such a lovely day. Thank you for coming," she said.

Jocelyn gave her mother a long, searching look, but made no reply, except to pat her shoulder.

A cold rain had begun to fall, and the early darkness had settled fully as Austin drove through the nearly empty streets. Jocelyn was quiet, and he felt no need to make conversation. Again he was struck by how comfortable it was to be with her, even though they disagreed on so many things. He decided it was because she felt no need to impress him. If ever he could declare love for her, he knew it must be in the same manner, completely accepting her as she was.

Aware of Jocelyn's presence in the seat next to him, and full of the intimacies of the day, he felt a growing urge to take her hand, to say something to her that would express how close he felt at this moment to her. But what? *I love you?* He dared not form the words.

Jocelyn had her own thoughts, and was lost in memories of her father. She saw him as a prince, a hero. On days like this, his absence was all the more poignant. It seemed so wrong that her mother should continue to live without him on the abundance he had provided, but in her heart she knew that thought was base and cruel. As angry as she was over her father's death, she had to admit, if only to herself, that her mother had grieved deeply, and had since shown her love and appreciation for the man.

Jocelyn only vaguely remembered the months of her parents' separation. More than the event, she remembered the fear and uncertainty. She remembered going with her parents to church, all the fun and excitement of Sunday school, and then the shattering death and return of the fears. As she had listened to Austin pray, she could almost envision her father at the table with them, his hearty bass voice saying, "Thanks, God! This is great! You really did it up in a big way for us."

She was drawn to the present by the touch of Austin's fingers against her own, but as she turned to look at him, she was blinded by the glare of lights. She saw Austin's face contort as he grabbed the steering wheel with both hands and pulled hard to the right. She felt the car spin around as the oncoming pickup truck clipped the rear fender. It sped away into the darkness as Austin's car careened into the median, bouncing and rocking all the way.

Instead of trying to stop, Austin forced himself to focus on the maze of lights and white lines around him in the darkness. Realizing the car was pointed in the right direction, he hit the accelerator and plowed through the wet grass of the median, then up the side and back onto the highway.

Jocelyn sat rigid, her hands gripping the edge of the seat. Austin slowed the car and stopped on the shoulder of the road.

"Are you all right?"

Jocelyn nodded. She was shivering. "Somebody came across the center line," she said.

"Yes."

"Your poor car."

Austin pulled his hand downward over his face, and stroked his beard a couple of times. "My poor car? My poor car? What about you?"

"I told you, I'm all right," said Jocelyn, and started to

cry. "I was so scared," she whispered, sniffling and shaking. "I was thinking about my dad. Then all of a sudden, there was that light. I thought I was going to die, Austin. I don't want to die. I'm not ready to die."

Gently he put his arm across her shoulders. "Neither am I," he said, remembering once again his feeble, empty prayer. Perhaps there had been Someone listening, and this was His way of saying He didn't appreciate half-wits like Austin presuming upon a relationship that didn't exist. "But we aren't going to die, Jocelyn. It's all right." Then he said something that he knew he could not have said three months ago. "The car doesn't matter."

"Let's go home," she said, drying her tears on the sleeve of the old jacket. "I just want to go home."

Austin drove out onto the street, and the rear wheel whined as it rubbed against the crushed metal. He stopped the car again, got out and pulled the fender away from the wheel, noting there seemed to be no other serious damage. He sent up another prayer of thanksgiving as he stood there in the darkness. This one came from the heart.

They rode in silence, Austin listening for telltale rattles or engine sounds that would signal damage, Jocelyn staring at her lap and opening and closing her fists. He stopped the car in her driveway and got out to open the door for her, and was startled when she stood up and hugged him securely around the waist.

"I really was afraid, Austin. Not just for me. For you, too." He could feel the tension in her body, and firmly wrapped his arms around her shoulders. He did not know what to say. Of the many adjectives he might use to describe this woman, "vulnerable" had never been one of them. Yet here she was, with none of the foot-stomping, head-tossing independence he had come to expect, no ready wit, no assurance that "it will all work out."

Jocelyn looked up at him and said, "What's going to happen to us? Where are we headed? I—"

For a fraction of a second, Austin thought she might say, "I need you," but she never completed her sentence. He thought of the day they had shared coffee, when she had stopped in midsentence just as he thought she was about to say, "I didn't think I needed anyone." She had never completed that sentence either.

"I don't know what's going to happen, but I know that when we are together, I am happier than at any other time. Trust me," he said, smiling at her, and borrowing her famous line. "It will work out." He held her close and felt her head nod against his chest. Together they walked to the door.

As Jocelyn opened the door, she turned a tear-streaked but now relaxed face to Austin. "Let's not tell Mom, all right?"

"About the accident?" he said.

"Anything," she answered. "Not just now. She had such a great day. I wouldn't want to spoil it for her."

"That's a good sign," said Austin. "Can it be you're beginning to think of your mother as human?"

Jocelyn toyed with the doorknob and did not look at Austin. "I know I've been tough on her, but it isn't as if I hate her."

Austin nodded. "I won't say anything."

She stepped inside. "Good night," she whispered.

He raised his hand. "Happy Thanksgiving."

five

December

As Austin left the small village market where he did most of his shopping, he saw Gerald Folkert on his way in.

"How's the photo business?" Austin called across the parking lot.

Gerald appeared startled, and looked around. Austin waved, but Gerald continued to look, as if he wondered whether anyone else might have heard the greeting. He walked quickly toward Austin.

"Hi," he said. "I'm just picking up a few things."

"I suppose those two kids eat a lot," said Austin.

"Kids. You mentioned them before." He frowned a moment, then laughed nervously. "The kids! Uh, they're with their mother," said Gerald. Austin nodded, and Gerald continued, "I see you visit Jocelyn Wentworth from time to time." Again Austin nodded, but thought it strange Gerald would be watching a neighbor that closely.

Gerald said, "I've been after her to let me do some portraits. I think she's got an interesting quality—sort of childish, you know?"

Austin didn't understand the wink Gerald offered, but he kept listening. Gerald handed him a business card that read, "Folkert Foto." The type was indistinct, and the card stock was cheap. Austin winced at the false alliteration and tucked the card into his shirt pocket.

"Put in a good word for me," said Gerald. "Have her give me a call. I think you'd be pleased with the results. She might be, too. I know she could use a little extra cash."

Austin became defensive. "She's very independent."

Gerald held up his hands and moved his head back a bit. "I only meant with Christmas coming, and all. Everybody can use a little extra at Christmas. It's honest work. Just tell her I talked to you. Put in a good word, OK?" He lightly jabbed a finger into Austin's upper arm, then walked toward the market.

Austin closed the trunk lid on his groceries. Once again, his gaze was drawn to the fender that had been wrecked Thanksgiving night. Though it was now repaired, the memory of that night was clear in his mind. Now, whenever he recalled the few seconds of crisis, they replayed in slow motion, and always his emotions churned, thinking of what might have happened.

He had not yet answered to his own satisfaction Jocelyn's questions. Where were they going? What would happen? He knew she was speaking about their relationship, and also about their lives in general. As he got into the car to go to the dry cleaning shop, Austin wondered if his life had actually peaked.

As he drove, Austin thought about the visit to the botanical garden last week. When he had told his father that Adelle Wentworth sent greetings, Martin had immediately called her. Austin, Jocelyn, Martin and Adelle had taken in the tropical display at the gardens, then had cappuccino and pastries in the adjoining cafe. Jocelyn had worn her dress-up sweat suit.

Adelle's grayed white silk blouse looked more expensive than it was because of its understated styling. She had paired it with pleated gabardine slacks and espadrilles, and thrown a soft, red-plaid wool scarf over her shoulder. Austin thought she might have been a New England matron, or a California executive, or an Arizona rancher. She seemed to be perfect for everything, and he wondered if any of Jocelyn's bitterness was envy of her mother's elegance.

Jocelyn had hugged Martin and welcomed him back to town, then linked arms with the two men while her mother walked to Martin's left. By the time they got to the coffee shop, Martin and Adelle were head-to-head, reminiscing about old times, not all of them happy.

His errands finished, Austin was heading toward his home when he came to the church both families had once attended. He had delivered the flyers advertising the Christmas concert here and had heard many enthusiastic endorsements. He glanced at his watch, saw it was not yet 5:30 P.M., and pulled into the long, winding driveway. He got to the office just as the secretary was about to lock the door.

"I was hoping I might have two tickets for the Christmas concert," he said, expecting a sullen response so late in the day.

"Oh, of course!" she exclaimed, unlocking the office door and going back inside. "I'm so glad you found me. Ordinarily I go home at 5:00, but I just couldn't get away today." She smiled warmly. "I guess the Lord just knew you were coming and needed these tickets. I only have one request. If for some reason you can't attend, please return them or just call and let us know. So many people want to come, but there just isn't room."

Austin reached for his wallet, then remembered the tickets were free of charge. "Thank you," he said. "I've heard many good things about the performance. I'm looking forward to it."

Since he was not far from Jocelyn's road, he went through a fast-food, drive-through restaurant, bought burgers, fries, and shakes, and went to her house. He knocked on the kitchen door.

"Hi!" she said, delighted at his unexpected appearance. "Is that fast food, I smell? Come in."

"I see you've been baking again," remarked Austin, noting the open oven door. "More cookies?"

"Oh, no, just taking the chill off the room. You know how these drafty old houses are. I was just thinking about supper." She cleared her pile of paperwork from the table and they sat down to eat.

Austin remembered Gerald Folkert's card. "I saw your neighbor today, and he asked me to let you know he's still interested in doing some photographs of you. He's willing to pay." He tossed the card onto the table.

Jocelyn nodded. "He came by the house a few days ago. He said he understood perfectly if I was nervous about coming to his house, and how he might have given me the wrong impression. He said he would make money from any photographs he sold, and he would pay me, too. He said he wanted everything open and aboveboard. He offered to bring his equipment here, if it would make me more comfortable. He said he had a contract from some playground equipment company and thought I'd be the perfect model."

"He did mention something about a childlike quality," Austin recalled.

"I'll think about it," she said. "Did you want that other burger?"

Austin passed her the extra food. "Jocelyn, will you go with me to the Christmas concert at the church? I hear it's quite a beautiful presentation. It would be a nice way to observe the holidays."

She hesitated, and he knew she was thinking about clothes. "Please come," he said. "If you can't go to church in comfortable clothes, where can you go? Surely God doesn't care what you wear."

"God isn't the only one at church," Jocelyn replied, "but you're right. I'd love to go. When is it?"

"Next week. I think our parents may also be going. Dad said something about it."

"Austin, I can't believe this! Our parents have had three dates since we went to the botanical gardens. Do you think they could be serious?"

Austin shrugged. "If they are, I don't know that there is anything we can do about it, or that we should try."

Jocelyn crumpled the burger wrapper tightly, using both hands. "I would hate to see my mother squelch your father, turn him into a suit-and-tie man."

"If she tried, she would have her work cut out for her," said Austin. "Someone like your mother deserves more dignity in a relationship than my father can offer."

"Well, it's probably nothing more than old friends getting reacquainted," said Jocelyn. "I mean, my mother couldn't have any romantic interests, not after—well, she must still remember my father."

"Don't you think people can love again after they lose someone?"

"Maybe. Oh, of course they do. People do it all the time. Someone dies and they go on, happy and comfortable just as though the person had never existed! But it isn't right."

"Do you think that's what your mother did?" he asked gently.

"Sometimes, yes, that's exactly what I think. I've never seen her cry even once since the funeral," said Jocelyn. "I think it was a relief to her when he died."

Austin stood up to leave. "I think you don't know your mother very well, and what's even more tragic is that you haven't allowed her to know you. You are so close, and yet you can't get together."

Jocelyn's voice had an edge of annoyance. "I don't see you winning any awards for parent-child relationships. Your dad is such a great guy. Why can't you appreciate him?"

Austin said nothing, but put on his jacket and walked toward the door.

"I'm sorry," Jocelyn apologized. "That was rude."

"Unless we want to have our first real fight," said Austin with a small smile, "we should probably drop this subject. I'll see you tomorrow."

The next day, Jocelyn was waiting at the mailbox, which she had trimmed with real holly from a shrub near the foundation of the old house. The long vines, covered with glossy green leaves, were wound around the posts, and a large red bow made from a discarded vinyl tablecloth adorned the door.

"Merry Christmas!" Jocelyn shouted, waving, as soon

as Austin drove near enough to hear her. He smiled and honked the horn, causing her to jump. It was the first time he had ever done something like that.

To add to the festive mood, there were checks for Jocelyn. Austin could usually recognize them now, and put them on the top of the pile whenever possible. Today there were three, but Austin never had any idea of the amount. He watched, satisfied, as her face registered her joy at the sight of the checks.

"Maybe I'll be able to give Christmas gifts," she said. It reminded Austin that he had not yet purchased a gift for Jocelyn, and in fact had not even firmly settled on what the right gift would be. He made a mental note to give her the gift after the program at church.

On the following Friday, Austin arrived at Jocelyn's home with a large box hidden in the trunk of his car. As he approached the house, Jocelyn flung the door open wide, and he was amazed to see her dressed in an ankle-length skirt of a woven material in a burgundy and pink floral design, and an oversized, high-collared pink blouse with sleeves that ballooned at the wrist. Her hair was pulled up into a bunch on top of her head, and she wore hoop earrings. She wore her trusty leather sandals with dark burgundy hose.

"I went shopping," Jocelyn chirped. "Greta told me that the Civic Theater was having their annual sale. They put out all the costume items they don't need. I got this outfit for seven bucks. It was worn by the star in *Meet Me in St. Louis*."

Austin slowly shook his head. "I don't know how you manage to always make something of nothing," he said. "I could almost believe in magic pumpkins and a fairy god-mother. You look lovely."

"Do you know what this concert will be like?" Jocelyn asked as they headed for the car.

"Not really," said Austin. "I've heard the decorating and lighting is quite spectacular, and there is a first-rate choir. Beyond that, I can't say. I would expect there will be traditional carols, maybe a pageant."

"I haven't been to church in a long time," Jocelyn said as they went down Greenwood. "After my father died, we didn't attend very often."

"Maybe it was difficult for your mother to be in those surroundings without him."

"I don't know. I only remember that for a while I missed my friends, because there was a whole different group of people there than at school. But, eventually, I just got busy doing other things. I graduated from high school, and people I had been aquainted with went away to college, or got married, or found jobs somewhere else." She shrugged. "I guess that's how it goes."

Austin nodded. "My father attended for a while after he and my mother broke up, but I stopped going with him. There was no reason, really. Like you, it just seemed easier. I wonder why we didn't meet at church?"

"You were too old," she said. "I was about twelve the last time I went to church. You would have been sixteen or so by then. We were in different worlds."

In different worlds! Jocelyn was struck by her own words. She and Austin were so different today, living such different lives, yet here they were together. Their childhoods had been similar, but their personalities were so different. Could there be any future for them? She was unsure herself whether she should pursue Austin and coax some kind of commitment from him. What she had at first thought was love might only have been infatuation. These friendly out-ings were pleasant, but the serious business of building a life together demanded agreement, if not conformity, on the most basic issues. How did Austin feel about marriage and children? She did not even know her own thoughts on those subjects, let alone his.

They entered the darkened auditorium to the strains of "The Coventry Carol" being played by a small orchestra sequestered near the large platform at the front.

"This is like an opera house!" Jocelyn whispered as they found their seats.

Austin shook his head. "You have to go to New York to find an opera house this big."

For Jocelyn, who had lived without television, movies, or even radio for many months, the music and special lighting, the drama and pageantry were a delicious treat to the senses. She relished every change of scene, drank in every solo and choral piece. The sheer beauty of the pro-duction overwhelmed her, and the thought that God loved her so much He sent His Son to live and then to die for her was deeply moving.

She had not thought of God in any personal way for many years. None of Aunt Bebe's Bible verses spoke directly about His intervention in the course of human events. Jocelyn certainly had felt no particular need to seek Him out. Yet here, in these surroundings, it was impossible to ignore Him.

Jocelyn stole a glance at Austin from time to time, and

saw his features drawn into a tense stare. He was listening carefully, judging the music, she assumed. Would it meet his discriminating standards? Still, he smiled at the right times, and during the Jamaican numbers, he could not keep from swaying with the soulful beat.

Then they stood and sang with the hundreds of others in the audience, "Joy to the World." Jocelyn thought surely the windows would shake loose as the orchestra and voices swelled with each succeeding verse. How long since she had sung that song? How long since Christmas had been special?

She sat with Austin as the people filed out of the room. "No point in hurrying," he said. "The parking lot will be jammed for half an hour."

"I should have brought my knitting," Jocelyn said.

"Do you knit?" he asked.

"Are you kidding? I don't do anything practical."

"But you do so many things beautifully," he said. "You bring grace to everything you touch."

"Austin, that is the nicest thing anyone has ever said to me."

He shifted in the seat, which was a bit too small for his large frame. "It's true," he said. "I want to talk to you about some important things, Jocelyn, but I can't seem to begin." He waved a hand to indicate the auditorium, now rather ordinary with the lights on. "All this has had an effect on me, and it concerns you—us. Can you be patient while I try to sort it out?"

She turned to look more directly at his eyes. "I will wait as long as you need me to wait. I can be patient if I put my mind to it."

The drive home was short, and the car had just begun to warm up when they returned to Jocelyn's house. Austin walked Jocelyn to the house and stepped inside. "It's cold in here!" he exclaimed. "What's wrong?"

"Oh, I turn the thermostat down low when I'm away," Jocelyn replied.

Austin frowned. "That's not really an economy measure. It uses more fuel to reheat the house than if you kept it at a low but steady temperature."

"I'll keep that in mind," Jocelyn said, not hurrying to take off her coat, and not touching the thermostat. "Come in the kitchen. It's warmer there. I'll make coffee."

"I'll be right there," Austin said. "I have to get something from the car."

When he returned, he was carrying a large box wrapped in white tissue with a plain red ribbon. He put it on the kitchen floor in front of Jocelyn and turned to her.

"I've thought so much lately about what I could give you that would be just right. I hope this is something that you can appreciate."

Jocelyn's face slowly brightened as she reached for the box. "Austin! Christmas is still a week away! I'm so surprised!"

Austin beamed as he sat down on the other chair and watched her open the box, carefully saving the ribbon. Jocelyn peeled off the package tape and opened the box to reveal two new snow tires.

"Tires? You got me tires for Christmas?"

He nodded, trying to rein in his smile. "They're top-quality snow tires. They'll last for years. You'll be able to drive your car again, Jocelyn. You'll have so much more freedom, and your car will be a lot safer, and in case of emergencies—"

She patted her closed lips with her fingers for a moment, then hauled one of the heavy tires out of the box, propped it on the floor, and stuck an arm through it.

"Wait until my mother hears you gave me a ring for Christmas," she said.

Slowly, Austin began to interpret her statement, and it dawned on him that he had committed a blunder of staggering proportions. He stared at Jocelyn as she hoisted the tire back into the box.

"I guess you might have liked something a little more personal."

"Hey, it's better than a lump of coal," Jocelyn said, then laughed and smiled at him. "Thank you, Austin. I know you thought about this a long time. I can't pretend I don't need the tires. And anyway, what would I do with silk or flowers or jewelry?" She wrinkled her nose in mock disdain, and Austin knew then that his gift was received in the spirit in which it was intended. The relief showed clearly on his face.

Jocelyn acknowledged to herself that she had secretly hoped Austin's gift would reveal some degree of intimacy. Apparently he was not ready, and Jocelyn had no indication that he ever would be ready. Or could it be that the only way he could communicate his feelings was through practical items and service? What was the message he was sending with the tires?

They sat together drinking coffee in the steadily cooling kitchen. When Austin went to the door, Jocelyn walked with him, her icy hands jammed in the pockets of her long skirt.

"Turn up the thermostat or your pipes will freeze," advised Austin. "It's supposed to get very cold tonight."

"My pipes won't freeze," said Jocelyn, patting her stomach. "I laced my coffee with antifreeze."

Austin laughed. "All right, I quit." Turning to go, he said with elaborate emphasis, "If I have your permission, I would like to come and get your car tomorrow and have the tires put on. May I?"

"Yes, you may, and thank you very much. I hope I didn't hurt your feelings. It's just that I wasn't expecting anything like—*snow tires!*" And she giggled. "You are a wonder."

"And I say again, you bring grace to everything you do, even when you are taken by surprise," he said. He placed his hands on her shoulders and looked into her eyes. "I asked you to be patient with me, but I also need you to trust me. There is so much I want to share, but—"

"I know," she said, and he felt the coldness of her fingers as she placed them on his lips.

Austin covered her hand with his own, gently passing the back of her fingers across his lips, then turning her hand to kiss the palm. As naturally as he had moved to the rhythm of the music earlier in the evening, he stepped toward her, pulling her close, and pressed his mouth against hers, still holding her hand against his chest.

For a long moment, Jocelyn felt her fears and strivings melt away, as though there really had been some drug in her coffee. She was at peace in Austin's arms more than she could ever remember. When she was a child and her frantic energy led her into one dissatisfying adventure after another, her father had cradled her in the big rocker in front of the fireplace and told her that someday she would be a princess, and that the world would be hers to command. But not even then had she experienced as much peace as tonight. Right now, this very moment, it was as if the world had finally come to her.

"I have to go," Austin said quietly.

She nodded. "I know."

"I'll see you tomorrow."

"Yes."

Austin walked through the unlighted yard to his car. The clear sky was a harbinger of cold weather, and his breath hung in the air, too chilled to move. As he started the car, shivering, and waited for the engine to warm, he knew there was another woman he had to deal with before he could say to Jocelyn what he now believed she wanted to hear.

six

January

Austin had always known where she was, of course, at least in general terms. And though they had exchanged correspondence on rare occasions, he had seen his mother only twice since the divorce, and had not communicated with her at all her after he entered the Air Force. Not that he hated her. He simply had no basis for interaction. He would not drop by to chat with his mother any more than he would his supervisor at the post office, or the teller at the bank.

A year plus a few months before he graduated from high school, she had left their home, and he had not known exactly why. His parents had sometimes argued in a polite way, but more often they had simply been disconnected from one another. Austin had tried to play peacemaker when they argued, and matchmaker when they were distant, but it was no use.

"These things happen," his father had said. "Adults have to make decisions about their lives, and you must not think she left because she doesn't love you." But Austin had always harbored the thought that had he or his father been more winsome or charming, they might have all stayed together.

Austin could only think that if he was not the problem, it

must be his father. Surely if his father had tried hard enough, had been willing to give up traveling or had spent more time in the social circles his mother enjoyed, then the marriage would have mended. When he found himself left with his father, he took it upon himself to take care of the details of the older man's life that seemed to have gone begging, like the yardwork and housekeeping. He even took an evening course in bookkeeping because he feared his father's business sense was inadequate.

As a child, he had appreciated his father's occupation, especially when his friends told him how much they envied him, living in a home where toys and games were the topic of conversation. After his parents' divorce, however, he saw his father's work as a symbol. The man invented toys because he was childish, irresponsible, afraid to grow up, Austin had reasoned, and that was probably why his marriage had failed.

Though Martin Van Doran had grieved visibly for the end of the most significant relationship in his life, he managed to go on living, and in a way, Austin resented it. He had always wondered if his father had done everything possible to win back his wife's affection. Austin had experienced so little failure in his own life that it was difficult for him to concede on any point.

Since the night he had kissed Jocelyn, he had been aware that the one thing keeping him from declaring his affection for her was his misgivings about marriage. It was so unmanageable, so dependent on two people working together. He had decided early on to take control of his own affairs, and to make a place for himself in the world where the unpredictable affections of others could not hurt him. He had largely succeeded, but he had found the place was also very lonely.

Before he could open his heart to Jocelyn, he knew he had to find out what had happened between his parents. And while he might make mistakes of his own, Austin could avoid repeating his parents' mistakes if he just knew what they were. Still, it had taken him several days to make the call to his mother and ask if he could come for a visit.

On New Year's Eve, he had brought Jocelyn to his home for the first time, and introduced her to some of his coworkers and a couple of college friends invited for the evening. It had been a stiff affair, but none of the fault lay with Jocelyn. She charmed everyone with her stories of people in the community and humor from her days in the dental office. Greta had come, too, and Jocelyn had gone home with her. Austin had hardly spoken to Jocelyn all evening except to say, "Happy New Year." He wondered all evening whether she was thinking about their Christmas kiss as much as he was.

He was thinking about Jocelyn as he stood at the door of his mother's home, wondering what he would say, wondering what she looked like. The last time he had seen her, he had been clean shaven. Would she recognize him? Could a mother fail to recognize her child?

The door opened, revealing a thin, tired-looking woman, who smiled at him. Sylvia Van Doran, now using her maiden name of Timmerman, stepped aside and said, "Come in, Austin. It's good to see you."

Austin stepped inside, seeing at once some of the old photographs from his childhood, even a favorite chair that was now reupholstered. "Hello," he said, hesitating to call her "Mother." It seemed too intimate.

"Come and sit down," she said. "Tell me what you've been up to these past few years. I heard you were back from college."

He nodded, taking a seat in a chair he recognized. "I'm with the post office. I started part-time downtown, then a full-time route opened up east of here. It's nice to be in the smaller station."

They chatted about his work, and her work, for a few minutes, and then Austin said, "I've met someone. I'm considering marriage."

Sylvia smiled broadly and slowly shook her head. "How like you to spend so much time considering! Have you made a list yet of how many things could go wrong?" Austin blinked, and had no reply. "I'm not criticizing," she said. "It's just that you've always been so terribly serious about everything. I just can't imagine you being in love. It's so—emotional."

He smiled self-consciously. "Well, that's one reason I came to see you. I do have a certain amount of hesitation about such a commitment. I've always wondered—well, I was young when you and Dad split up, and I never really understood what happened. I need to know."

Sylvia settled back on the sofa. "Didn't your father ever explain it to you?"

"He would only say that as adults, people are responsible for their own lives and must make the decisions they think are best. I assumed you just didn't love each other anymore."

Sylvia tapped her fingers on the sofa cushion and looked

at the ceiling. "Your father may not be everything you or I wanted him to be, but he is kind. Austin, our marriage began to fail for a lot of reasons. The only thing I can say is that it just fell apart. It was like a garden that doesn't get proper attention. Weeds grow up. There isn't enough water or nutrients for the good plants that are there, and they die. You have to work at a marriage. We didn't. We had something good at one time, but we let it slip."

She shifted her gaze so that she was speaking to the window and continued. "Actually, I met someone else that I thought was a little more exciting than Martin." Austin felt his stomach churn and the muscles of his neck tighten. His mother continued, "He was just a friend. We used to chat on the phone, have coffee together, talk about books and things we were interested in. When I found I was beginning to look forward to your father's trips so I could spend more time with him, I knew the marriage was in trouble."

"Didn't Dad ever ask you to go along on the trips? Didn't you ever want to be with him?"

"Your father tried to include me in his life, just as he tried to include you. But it takes effort and change to appreciate someone who isn't like you. Now, I think I was sort of lazy. And maybe he was a little bit stubborn in his own way. I don't know. It's been a long time."

"Don't you ever think about getting back together? Have you ever discussed it with Dad? You said you had something good once. Maybe you could find—"

"We tried for a while," she said, "but we were different people then."

"The church membership years?"

She nodded. "It was a funny thing. Your dad seemed to get some real insight about his own life during those years, but I had pretty well decided by then it was over. He wanted me to keep going to church even after we separated. He said it wasn't just for his sake, but for mine. He said I needed to let God have His way in my life. I think that's what happened to him. I think he had some kind of spiritual awakening. I didn't understand it." She shrugged. "That would have been work, too, and even more change. I just wanted to have it done with." She looked directly at Austin and said in a tone that was solid and almost cold, "You need to understand, Austin, we didn't 'split up.' I left him."

"But couldn't you go back now?" Austin asked, hearing the longing in his own voice.

Sylvia looked at Austin directly now. "Austin, I married the other man."

Austin knew his mouth was open, but he couldn't seem to do anything about it except pull his lips together, then let them go slack again.

"I asked your father not to tell you," said Sylvia, now looking away. "I thought it would be best for you if you just got on with your life and didn't have any fantasies about my coming back. I stepped out of your life because I felt it would be better for you. Maybe I was wrong."

In response to Austin's dumbfounded silence, she said with some irritation, "You were practically an adult, you know. My new husband wasn't interested in having a teenager call him 'Dad.' Believe me, keeping it from you was for your own best interests."

Austin's mind was reeling. "You're married? When? Your name—"

"We were married shortly after you went away in the service," she said. "I kept using my maiden name because people in town knew me by that name."

Austin felt hot, and he took shallow breaths to control his voice. "I see. So the answer is, just find the right person? Make sure you don't lose interest? Keep dating, that kind of thing?"

Sylvia now looked even more tired than before. "The answer, Austin, is don't ask me. Ask someone who has the kind of marriage you want to have. If you're set on that once-in-a-lifetime thing, be ready to take some hard knocks. I didn't need that. Life's hard enough without depriving yourself of a back door." She turned away from Austin and began adjusting the flowers in the silk arrangement on the coffee table. "Actually, my husband and I are separated right now. I don't know if we'll get back together." She shrugged. "He might even be seeing someone else."

Sylvia got up and walked to a bookcase where photo albums were stacked. "If you think you might be getting married, I'll give you this now. It's you, your childhood and high school years. You might want to keep it to show to your own children."

Austin still could think of nothing to say as he accepted the album.

"Don't be too hard on me," Sylvia said. "And don't be too hard on yourself. You always wanted everything perfect. Well, things aren't perfect. People aren't perfect."

"But just because things—and people—aren't perfect, does it make it all right to walk out?" he asked.

She shrugged again. "That's the decision you have to make. What's done is done. I'm not the only one, you know. Marriage is only a fifty-fifty chance anyway. I hope it works for you."

Austin resisted the temptation to lash out at her. Something inside told him her remarks were designed to diminish her own guilt, and that she had never fully accepted her part in the divorce. At least she had been honest with him to the limit of her own understanding. He left the house shaken, saddened, disappointed, and with no more knowledge of how to guarantee a lasting marriage relationship than he had before. But if you couldn't learn such facts from your mother, who could you turn to?

&

Jocelyn hurried down the road, the wind in her face. She had been to visit Greta and had stayed a little too long. The late afternoon sun had begun to set, taking with it the warmth that would have made the walk home tolerable. A cardinal flew across the road, and the sight lifted Jocelyn's spirits. She made a mental note to buy some sunflower seeds to put out as soon as she could afford it. Tracing the path of the bird, Jocelyn did not notice a black pickup truck coming along behind her.

"Hey, how about a lift?" Gerald Folkert called when he came beside her.

Jocelyn eyed him warily for a moment, but the chilling breeze convinced her to accept the ride.

"Thanks," she said, opening the passenger door. "Greta's car is in the shop and she couldn't give me a ride home. I love the walk when the sun's out, but it's getting pretty cold now that the clouds have rolled in."

"Glad I came along," said Gerald, letting the truck coast along. "Say, did the mailman give you my message? About making a little extra money? I'm always looking for people to model."

"He mentioned it, and gave me your card. I just got busy. What kind of photography do you do?"

"Commercial," he said. "Calendars and things like that for businesses."

"Well, I appreciate the offer, but really, I can't imagine seeing my face on the wall next to the coffee machine every day for a month. I just don't think I'd be comfortable with the idea, but thanks anyway."

To Jocelyn's surprise, Gerald turned in to his own driveway and drove up to the house. To her questioning look, he said, "I just thought I'd show you some of my work and maybe change your mind. New faces are what make my business successful. Come on in."

"I'd really rather go home. I can walk from here." She reached for the door, but as she climbed out, so did he, coming around to meet her.

"Jocelyn, we're neighbors," he said, smiling and holding the door open for her. "I'll be very hurt if you don't come in and take a look at my work. Even if you aren't interested, you can do me a big favor by recommending other people you know. You're a popular girl. You must have plenty of friends." He nodded in the direction of the house, and for a moment, Jocelyn wavered. He was a neighbor, after all.

But there was something odd about how earnestly he was trying to persuade her. She had not gotten this far in life without learning to trust her instincts. In a sudden movement, she shoved the door into him so that he lost his balance and fell backward onto the driveway, cursing as he went.

Jocelyn ran down the driveway as fast as she could. She heard Gerald yelling crude, disgusting phrases after her, but she didn't look back. She was afraid he would get back into the truck and come after her. She breathed a sigh of relief when she reached the end of the driveway and the pickup had not moved. When she got home, she locked her doors for the first time since she had lived in Aunt Bebe's house.

ᕉ

Austin sighed as he saw the large envelope sticking out of Gerald Folkert's box. The morning snow had covered the exposed end and Austin knew it would be soggy, and possibly torn. As he pulled the envelope from the box, Austin saw that once again Gerald had forgotten to write a return address on it. Austin had mentioned the problem to him several times before, but Gerald had always shrugged, as if he didn't care that the postal service would not be able to return a misdirected package to him.

Austin decided to jot a quick return address on the corner of the envelope. "Like I've got time for this," he muttered to himself. As he started to write, the point of his pen ripped the soggy envelope and Austin found himself staring at the photographs inside. In a moment, he realized he had been a fool.

The photos of young women were obviously not done in a professional studio, but Austin knew there was a big market for them. The hopeful looks on the faces of the young models told him they had been promised that posing for these immoral, degrading photographs would be the first step to a wonderful career. Gerald probably told them they would be sought after as serious models by sophisticated advertising firms, and that this kind of work was just the first rung on the ladder, the place where all models started.

"She's got an interesting quality—kind of childish," Gerald Folkert had said about Jocelyn. Austin's heart raced at the thought that he had encouraged her to contact the man. The thought of them together, of Gerald talking to her, lying to her, trying to persuade her to do something so evil made him sick.

"I believe that's private," said Gerald Folkert. Austin was startled to see the photographer standing next to the mail truck with another oversized envelope in his hand.

"You know this is illegal," Austin replied, a steely note in his voice. I'm taking this to the postmaster."

Gerald offered his most winning smile. "Why don't you just forget about this? You know this goes on all the time. I'm not hurting anyone. Everyone's an adult here, just having a little fun and making a few bucks on the side."

"Oh?" said Austin. He held up a photo of the little boy and girl he had seen in Gerald's yard. They were scantily clothed, looking frightened and bewildered. Austin knew it was just the kind of photo designed to make a pornography addict beg for more explicit material. "When were you going to bring these two 'adults' back for another session?"

Gerald looked apprehensive. "Hey, they've got clothes on. There's nothing wrong with those. Just give 'em back to me and we'll forget the whole thing."

Austin shook his head, but Gerald made a lunge for the material, grabbing it away and running across the road back toward his house. In a second, Austin was after him, tackling him and throwing him into the ditch on the side of the road. He couldn't let the photos be destroyed. He grabbed for Gerald's arm to bring it behind his back and immobilize him, but the man got off a solid punch that landed just below Austin's left eye. Austin reeled backward as Gerald grabbed the photos again.

Austin scrambled to his feet and lunged at Gerald from behind, grabbing him around the neck, and pulling his arm behind his back.

"You're killing me!" Gerald screamed. "Let me go! You can have the pictures."

Austin walked Gerald back to the Jeep and shoved him up against the side of the vehicle. He maintained pressure on the photographer's arm, but relaxed his grip slightly as he reached for his cell phone to call the police. Gerald seized the opportunity and spun away from Austin's grasp. This time he headed straight for his truck, jumped in, and raced down the driveway, turning west onto Greenwood. Austin carefully explained the situation to the 9-1-1 dispatcher, who promised to send the police in pursuit of Gerald. Suddenly, Austin realized that Gerald had driven off in the direction of Jocelyn's house. He scrambled back into his Jeep and raced down Greenwood Road.

The sight of Jocelyn at the mailbox, a bright red band around her head to cover her ears and a steaming cup in her hand made him want to jump out and wrap his arms around her. She was safe.

"Wow! What's the big hurry around here today?" she asked. "I just saw Gerald Folkert zoom by like he was late to a fire, and now you drive up like you're being chased by wolves. What's going on?"

When Austin explained what had happened, Jocelyn grabbed his arm. "See? See? I told you he was creepy, didn't I? He tried to make me come into his house just yesterday. I can't believe it!" Suddenly her face took on a stricken expression. "Austin! You said you saw children there."

"Gerald said they were gone and I believe it. I've never seen them any other time. I think he was just setting himself up for some fast cash. Serious pornography takes a lot of effort. Guys like him are too lazy to make it pay."

"You sound like an expert."

"You can't get through military service without getting an education about what's available on the street." He dropped his head into his hands. "How could I have been so blind?"

Jocelyn patted him on the arm. "It's all right," she said. "I'm so proud of you. The post office will probably give you a medal."

Austin did not get a medal, but he received a certificate of appreciation from his station supervisor, a letter of commendation from the regional postmaster, and a bonus in his next paycheck.

He had trouble sleeping the next few nights. That he had been so easily deceived weighed heavily on his mind. That Gerald Folkert had tried to exploit Jocelyn made him angry all over again. His anger simmered, even though he knew Folkert had been arrested almost immediately and would be arraigned in a few days. The thought of Jocelyn's vulnerability in the old house gnawed at him. He knew he had to discuss marriage with her. The next time he saw her at the mailbox, he asked to see her that evening.

٭

The first thing Austin noticed when he entered the house was how cold it was.

"Have you been playing with the thermostat again?" he demanded.

She shooed him into the kitchen where the oven door was open. "Just sit down here. It's warm enough. I just cover the kitchen door with a blanket and turn the oven on for a half hour every now and then, and I can live with it. We always get a warm spell in January, and February is only twenty-eight days long, and then it's March. Winter's over. I'll make it."

Austin's frustration was evident. "Jocelyn, are you telling me you have no source of heat in this house? You can't live this way!"

"But I do," she said, "and quite well, actually. Here, have some tea. It warms you up. Sorry, the coffee's all gone."

"And your plumbing? Have you shut off the water?"

She shook her head and took a long drink of tea. "I have a little space heater in the cellar that keeps it warm enough so the pipes don't freeze. And I have plenty of hot water, so if I get really cold, I take a shower, or do some laundry by hand." She set the cup down on the table. "There's a good furnace in the house. It's old, but it works—I think. The trouble is it uses oil, and the tank is empty. The company won't deliver just a few dollars worth, like $25 or $50. You have to fill the tank, and I just haven't been able to get that kind of cash together. It would cost about $200. I'll just get along the way I have been."

"Jocelyn, please let me give you—or at least loan you— the money. I can't stand seeing you like this."

"Like what?" she asked emphatically. "Do I look like I'm suffering?" At a glance, Austin could see that Jocelyn was wearing most of the clothing she owned—the smaller red flannel shirt covered by the larger blue one, topped with the old sweatshirt. She was wearing jeans, but Austin could see at the cuffs the telltale edge of sweatpants worn underneath. Her feet looked like shapeless lumps of dough because of the layers of socks, and as she sat at the table, she had the comforter over her shoulders.

"You look like a bag lady," he said.

"I've heard they make a good living."

"Jocelyn, I came over to talk to you about something important, something serious. I've been thinking about this a lot." He hesitated, afraid to speak the words for fear she might say no, or maybe because she might say yes. "We haven't spent a lot of time talking about our feelings, but I know I want to always be available to you, to give you what I can. Jocelyn, would you consider marrying me?"

She did not smile, and Austin's heart sank.

After a pause, she said, "You didn't say the magic word," and stared into her cup.

Austin thought a moment. "Please?"

"Sorry," she said softly, "that only works with your mother. Austin, you just feel sorry for me. You want to take care of me, to get me to shape up and live normally and be another ornament in your beautiful house."

"No! No, Jocelyn, I would never ask you to change. Of course, I want to share what I have with you, but I've come to appreciate your strength of character. Only someone as independent as you could have broken away from Gerald Folkert that way. You're a wonderful person."

"And?"

"And. . .and. . .I want you to marry me, Jocelyn."

"You asked me to consider it, and I will," she said. But there was no enthusiasm in her answer. "How about some more tea?"

"That's all? When will you know? Jocelyn, I'm asking you to marry me! This is a big step for me."

"Yes, I know. It is for me, too."

Austin thought how selfish his response must have sounded. "I didn't mean that it was only for me, just that I've thought a lot about it, and because of some doubts and problems that, well, it's taken a long time and—"

"Stop, Austin," Jocelyn said in the same quiet tone. "I said I'd consider it. But can't you understand?" She leaned close to him, and placed her hand on his. "I don't want you to take care of me. I just want you to care."

seven

February

The howling wind had continued all night long, and Austin knew he was in for a rough day. Yesterday's snowstorm had escalated to near-blizzard conditions this morning, and he put on his warmest clothing, thinking all the time of Jocelyn in her freezing cold house. He left his house at 4:30 A.M. and crept along the highway toward the post office. Even the semis were traveling at less than forty miles per hour.

Mary Ellen was already at the station when Austin arrived.

"Did you sleep here?" he asked.

"Just about," she answered. "I guess none of us needed to hurry. The truck from downtown isn't here yet."

"You mean I could have stayed in bed another hour?" Irritated, Austin hung up his jacket and went to make coffee. If he and Mary Ellen could be on time, others should be, too.

He was nearly an hour late starting his route, and the roads were slippery and filled bank to bank with snow. Plows had been busy all night just keeping main roads open. Six inches of new snow had fallen since midnight, the temperature was down to eight degrees, and the wind had increased. Austin clamped his jaws together and drove with determination. He had known there would be days like this. Now he just wanted to get through this one.

He was amazed to find Jocelyn waiting for him at the mailbox, two warm triangles of shortbread and fresh coffee in her hands.

"Jocelyn, this is lovely," he said, "but you should be back inside. You aren't even wearing any boots."

In the minutes she had waited at the box, Jocelyn's tracks from the house already had filled with blowing snow. She squinted against the snow being driven into her face and her voice rose slightly to compensate for the wind.

"I wanted to see you," she said. "I know you've been worried, and I just wanted to let you know I'm ordering fuel oil today. I got a fat check from that dog food company for naming their official puppy. You know, the one that has the hunk of postman's uniform hanging out of his mouth? I'm all right. Don't worry."

Austin smiled and nodded vigorously. "That makes me feel a lot better," he said. "You just can't get along without heat in this kind of weather."

Jocelyn handed him a slip of paper on which she had written the name of a fuel supply company and the phone number, and the words "one hundred gallons."

"Would you mind calling the company for me?" she asked. "I don't want to walk to Greta's today."

"It will be my pleasure," said Austin. He put the paper into his jacket pocket, then thought of something. "Do you know how to light the furnace?"

"I asked my mother about it. She came over to help Aunt Bebe during the last winter she lived here. That was almost two years before she died. Mom explained it to me, and I went downstairs and looked it over. I think I've got a handle on it."

"Well, I'll ask the delivery driver to make sure it's operating properly before he leaves," said Austin. "That is, if you don't mind."

Jocelyn grinned. "I'm not that proud."

"I'm late. I've got to go." He eased the truck back into the trackless road, and Jocelyn turned toward the house. Suddenly, Austin hit the brakes, leaned out, and yelled above the wind, "What did you name the puppy?"

She grinned and called back, "Stamper!"

That night, the sky cleared and the temperature plummeted to eleven degrees below zero. Austin had been assured by the fuel company that a delivery truck would be at Jocelyn's home by 7:00 A.M. the next morning, but when he awakened at 4:00 A.M. and saw the thermometer on the side of his house, he hoped she was wearing flannel pajamas.

The main roads were clear and Austin hurried to the station and through the loading in order to get to Jocelyn's home as soon as possible. He was gripped by a sense of urgency and apprehension, though he knew the fuel oil was on its way.

He felt some relief when from the top of the hill on Greenwood just beyond Greta's house, he could see smoke rising from the chimney on Jocelyn's house. As he pulled up to the mailbox, he noted the tracks of the delivery truck in the snow that covered the driveway. She was all right.

He began stuffing the mailbox, but the sense that something was wrong nagged at him. Then he realized there was no mail in the box. Jocelyn would have brought her daily collection of entries to the box by now, or would have met him. There were no tracks from the house.

Austin turned again and looked at the smoke coming from the chimney. Suddenly, he jumped from the truck and ran to the house, hoping every second to see Jocelyn's face peeking through the curtains. She did not appear. There was no sense of movement, no sign of life.

Before he opened the door, Austin could smell the sickening fumes of the defective fuel oil furnace. He tried not to breathe, knowing the odor was the least dangerous factor. Deadly carbon monoxide was seeping into every room.

He headed directly for the kitchen and found Jocelyn slumped over the table, still dressed in layers of clothing, her comforter wrapped around her. He imagined her lighting the furnace after the fuel oil had been delivered, then coming back upstairs to work while the house warmed. Austin lifted her from the chair and headed for the kitchen door. The room was warm, but he felt the coolness of her cheeks as he bent to try to detect breath. Why hadn't she left the house? Austin had never considered the danger of a cracked fire wall when she said she was going to start heating the house. A newer gas furnace, he knew, might emit carbon dioxide from a defective exhaust system or cracked fire wall and there would be no warning odor. With fuel oil, however, the noxious smell should have alarmed Jocelyn.

Austin carried her down the back steps and toward the old Lincoln. He got the back door open and laid her on the seat, willing her to breathe. He placed his fingers against the clammy skin of her throat, searching for a pulse, and felt his own quicken when he detected a faint, irregular beat.

"Jocelyn," he said clearly. She turned her head a fraction of an inch, her eyes still closed.

"Wake up," he said, "you've overslept." She lay still, but he could see now that she was taking shallow breaths. "You have to wake up," he said, louder. "You'll miss the mail!"

Jocelyn's eyes opened a crack, and she struggled to move, but could not. Austin pulled her upright, then lifted her in his arms so she could be out of the car in the cold, crisp air.

"Cold," she whispered.

"It's good for you," said Austin. "Breathe, Jocelyn. Keep breathing. Please, keep breathing."

Once again he placed her on the backseat of the Lincoln, covered her with his own jacket, and ran to the mail truck to get his phone.

It seemed like it took forever, but six minutes after Austin's call, an ambulance pulled into Jocelyn's driveway. Austin watched anxiously as the paramedics administered oxygen and loaded the semiconscious Jocelyn into their van.

"I'll be there as soon as I can," Austin said, "just as soon as I can get there."

"Mail must go," she muttered, her lips still blue, and Austin was thrilled. He knew that she recognized him.

"I'll call your mother," he said. He watched the doors of the ambulance close and thought there was something else he should say, but he could not think of it.

Adelle Wentworth was sitting beside her daughter when

Austin arrived that afternoon. He dragged a chair from across the room and sat beside her.

"What's the prognosis?" he asked.

"Everyone is saying she will be all right."

They sat together silently, watching the unnaturally still form of their dear Jocelyn. Both Austin and Adelle wondered what they might have done to prevent this disaster, but there were no easy answers.

Anxious questions raced through Austin's mind. What if the storm had continued another few hours? What if he would have arrived later, as he had the previous day? What if he would have dismissed his apprehension and driven on? What if she would have died?

As Austin watched her quiet, relaxed breathing as she slept, he had the feeling she had been given back to him, and he felt a deep sense of gratitude. He remembered the accident on Thanksgiving night and decided that God must be involved in these brushes with death. He remembered Jocelyn's words that night: *"I'm not ready to die."*

At the time, Austin assumed Jocelyn had been talking about the deplorable state of her business and personal affairs. Now he thought perhaps she had been talking about a spiritual dimension that they had never discussed. He remembered how they both had pretended not to notice each other's reaction to the Christmas concert performance. They should have talked then about the meaning of it all, but he had rushed ahead with his marriage proposal, too bent on his own agenda to think about Jocelyn's needs beyond material comfort.

As he looked at the monitors and blinking lights around him, Austin silently vowed to begin building a spiritual foundation for their relationship, even though he had no clue at that moment how it should be done. He only knew that his parents and Jocelyn's had come to the point where they realized it was the key to their survival. Austin would not wait until it was too late for Jocelyn and him.

Adelle took a deep breath and slowly exhaled, as if she were very tired. She turned to Austin and said, "I will never be able to thank you enough, Austin, for everything you have done for her."

"She might have died," he said quietly.

Adelle nodded. "Yes, and I don't believe she is ready."

Austin was startled. "She said that to me. Thanksgiving night, after the accident."

"What accident?"

Austin looked away. "It was minor," he said, "and Jocelyn didn't want you to worry. We were hit by a car that night, and though we were quite shaken, the only damage was to the fender of my car. But she said, 'I'm not ready to die.' I was just thinking about that night, and thinking that we need to look more deeply at spiritual issues. I've been so concerned with getting everything in order for this life, I haven't thought much about the next, and I do believe death is not the end of it all."

"You're right, it isn't," said Adelle. "That was the realization my husband and I came to not long before he died. Those two years, when we both had our sights fixed on a higher purpose than our own comfort, were the best of our life together. Maybe that's why Jocelyn's rejection has been so hard to bear. Her father and I both tried to share what had happened to us, but she wasn't ready. She loved us—especially her father—as we had been. She didn't want to hear about change. I think she was always threatened by it, so I stopped pushing."

Austin remembered his own mother's response. Change was difficult, she had said. She, too, had chosen to go a different direction than follow the new path chosen by her husband. What if Jocelyn responded that way, too?

Adelle put her hand on Austin's forearm and said, "If you care about Jocelyn at all, please don't turn her against me any further."

"I'll do everything I can to mend the rift," promised Austin, "but I'm beginning to think it will take something bigger than both of us to do that. I don't know—well, I'm not sure how Jocelyn feels about me, how much she is influenced by my opinion." He stopped short of telling Adelle about the proposal of marriage.

She nodded. "I think you are a wise man, Austin, and good for Jocelyn. But if I told her that, it would be the kiss of death on your relationship, so I'm staying out." She smiled and patted his arm a moment, then stood up to leave. "The nurse said she would probably be asleep for most of the evening. I'm going home. I'll come back about 10:00 P.M. Stay if you like, but she probably doesn't know you're here."

"Thanks, I'll stay a while." He sat alone through the evening, watching her sleep, thinking of the events of the last few months and wondering whether she would really be all right. Would she suffer some lingering effect of the gas? Would she have memory loss, or impaired motor control? *She will need me all the more,* he thought, and he resolved to be there for her in any capacity. And in the far recesses of his mind, he wondered, *Is this love?*

ða

Jocelyn was enjoying a second helping of pancakes and sausage the next morning when the hospital chaplain came into her room.

"Good morning," he said. "I'm Reverend Mark Sweeney. May I visit with you a moment?"

"Oh, sure," said Jocelyn, jabbing a fork in the direction of the chair. "These pancakes are so good! I hope you don't mind if I finish. I can talk and eat without being disgusting."

Mr. Sweeney laughed. "I'd say from the looks of things that you are feeling fine this morning. You weren't quite so talkative last night."

Jocelyn shook her head slowly from side to side. "What a scary thing! Something inside told me I should get out of the house when it began to smell so bad, but it was so cold, I didn't want to go out." She scooted sideways in the bed until she faced the man directly. "Before I lighted that furnace, I looked inside, and I could see where squirrels or mice or something had built a nest, so I pulled the stuff all out. Then when I noticed the smell, I just figured there was another nest higher up somewhere that I hadn't seen. I figured it would go away after the fire had been going a while." She leaned back against the pillows. "That was close."

"Yes, it was," agreed Mr. Sweeney. "You have a wonderful opportunity, Miss Wentworth. Not everyone gets a second chance. Have you thought about how you will live your life now?"

"It's a funny thing," she said. "On Thanksgiving night, my friend and I were hit by an oncoming pickup. I was so scared. I thought I was dead right there, and I told him

I wasn't ready to die. I knew it. After that, I thought my life would be so different, because—like you said—I had a second chance. But, somehow, it goes on the same. Now it's happened again. Do you think I should move to Tibet or something? Strive for wisdom? Dedicate my life to the poor like Mother Teresa? I don't see myself living that way."

He smiled and shook his head. "No, that seems uncharacteristic, but I think you have acquired some insight. You've given some thought to your own death, something a surprising number of people avoid completely. The fact is, we all die. The only unknowns are when and how. Tell me, what do you think happens after death?"

Jocelyn thought of the Sunday school lessons she had heard, the cartoons picturing people in white robes with halos, the fearful predictions of television evangelists about judgment. "I think—though I'm not certain—that we will be accountable to God for our lives. There must be some different plan for good people than for bad people, but I wouldn't want to be on the committee to decide who's good and who's bad."

Mr. Sweeney chuckled at Jocelyn's forthright answer. "Fortunately, for all of us, God reserves that job for Himself, according to the Bible. It isn't such a difficult choice as we humans make it out to be. We read in Isaiah 53:6 that we have all gone astray, we have all gone out of the way—the way that leads to God—and are really good for nothing. That's everyone. No difference. We all deserve to be separated forever from the perfect holy God."

"But is that fair?" Jocelyn asked. "I know I'm not perfect, but. . .well, my neighbor, Gerald Folkert, you don't want to know what he did. He's in jail right now."

"The first thing we must do if we want to have eternal life," explained Mr. Sweeney, "is to look at sin as God does. He is perfect. Only perfection is acceptable to Him, so we're all guilty. To the degree our sins affect others, He will judge, of course, but in ourselves, we have nothing to offer Him."

"But doesn't the Bible say Jesus died to pay the price for sin?"

"Yes, it does," said Mr. Sweeney. "One of the most loved verses in the Bible, John 3:16, tells us that. Have you ever reached out in faith and said to God that you accept His free gift of salvation?"

Jocelyn thought of the prayers of her childhood, of snatches of conversation with her parents and Aunt Bebe. "It doesn't make any sense," she had often said. God seemed too far away, and she didn't want to think about Jesus' death. Most of all, she had never wanted to admit that she needed anything from anybody, even from God.

Now here I am, she thought. *My house is unlivable, my car undriveable, my work interrupted, my bank account empty, my cupboard bare. Who am I kidding?*

"I think I always figured that just wasn't for me," she said to Mr. Sweeney. "I hate to admit it, but it was mostly pride."

"You are not alone. It is pride that keeps all of us from enjoying the grace God offers for living, and for dying. This time you lived to tell about your experience. But what about next time? When it is time to enter eternity, will you argue with God and say you are doing all right on your own?"

"No," she said quietly. "I know you're right." The memory of Aunt Bebe's faith now made sense to Jocelyn. She had explained to Jocelyn on different occasions how God had bridged the gap between Himself and man through Jesus Christ. That was why she was in communion with God. She had crossed the bridge. "I have to make a change," Jocelyn said, "and I'm going to start right now."

ঌ

Seeing that her normal enthusiasm had returned was a great relief to Austin. He had wondered what he might find when he returned the next day, and he was thrilled to see her completely rejuvenated.

"Hello," he said brightly, laying down the bouquet of roses he had brought. "I'm glad to see you.

Suddenly, Jocelyn was overwhelmed with the significance of Austin's presence. She held her arms out to him. Austin leaned in for a hug.

"You rescued me again," she murmured into his shoulder. "Where will it ever end?"

"It doesn't have to," Austin answered, letting her go. "Are you really all right?"

She nodded. "I've been up walking around and they did a bunch of tests. But if you hadn't been there. . .well, I guess I would have died." She explained why she had not left the house, and Austin again berated himself for not being more careful about the furnace.

"Austin, I talked to the hospital chaplain today. I've learned something. I think the secret of Aunt Bebe's practical religion was she knew everything was settled. She understood what God wanted from her, and as I understand it, He doesn't want anything except acceptance and faith. I've always known about God, but I wasn't connected to Him. Now I know it was my pride—sin—that separated us. Am I making any sense?"

Austin hesitated. "Yes, a little. I've been thinking along those lines myself, after everything that's happened."

"Well here, take these," Jocelyn said, bundling a collection of pamphlets and a Bible left by the chaplain into his hands. "I'll get some more tomorrow from the chaplain."

Austin tucked the books into his coat pocket and removed a small box.

"I'll bet you don't know what day it is," he said.

Jocelyn thought briefly. "Tuesday. It's February 14. It's Valentine's Day."

He smiled and handed her the box.

"It's too small to be a tire," she said teasingly, shaking it. "Let me guess. Dental floss?"

"All right, I deserved that. Open it."

Jocelyn tore off the paper and found inside the box a pair of earrings similar to those she had borrowed from Greta, but much more expensive. She put them on immediately.

"Do they match my gown?" she asked, pulling at the flimsy cotton hospital garment.

"They match you," said Austin. "Jocelyn, I know now what has been missing from our discussions. I've never told you how much I love you. That was the magic word, wasn't it? You wanted to hear me say it. Well, I'm saying it, right out loud. I love you, Jocelyn. I want to marry you."

Jocelyn's face took on a serene but wistful expression. *If only he had said that a week ago!* she thought. "It's exactly what I wanted to hear," she said quietly, "but—"

"But? I hate that word," he said.

"Austin, right now, after all this, I can't say yes. I don't want to say 'I love you' when I might just mean 'thanks a lot for saving my life.' "

He took an audible breath, placed his hands on his knees and straightened up in the chair. "I see. All right. There's time. The important thing is for you to get well, and—"

"And you'll be here for me. For the first time, I can say that really makes me happy."

"Then we're on the right track, aren't we?" He touched her cheek, and she placed her hand over his. "Adelle told me you would be going to stay with her."

"It's not as if I have any choice," she replied. "You know what they say. Home's the place where, when you have to go there, they have to take you in."

eight

March

Jocelyn suffered from headaches and general exhaustion, and the doctors told her it would be several weeks before she could consider herself completely recovered from her ordeal. Though she hated living at her mother's house again, she tried to set aside the behavior that she herself had called "bratty."

Jocelyn spent her days resting, reading, and trying to determine what she should do.

"You don't have to do anything," insisted Adelle. "You know you can live here as long as you like, and any work you choose will be fine with me. You don't have to prove anything."

"Only to myself," said Jocelyn.

One evening, Jocelyn turned off the television, bored with the programming. "I haven't missed anything by not having a TV," she remarked to her mother, who was writing letters. Jocelyn began looking through some photo albums that were tucked into a bookshelf. "Mom, did you do these?" she asked, looking at the artfully designed pages. "They're great."

"I took one of those classes a couple years ago while you were at the junior college. It's one of those things I kept thinking I should do, and just finally did it. You would enjoy that, Jocelyn, with your creative abilities. I just copied the instructor's designs, but if you like, you can do an album yourself. I still have boxes of photographs and materials for doing the pages."

As the two worked on the project, they got reacquainted, and Jocelyn gained a new appreciation for her mother. Adelle spoke lovingly about Jocelyn's father—how he had loved his work, his wife, and his daughter. He had simply died too young. No one was to blame. Jocelyn began to believe that her mother had truly loved and appreciated Michael Wentworth. And both women missed him.

Jocelyn was beginning to feel reconciled to her mother when Adelle dropped a bombshell. "You know that I have been seeing Martin Van Doran, right? Well, he and I are seriously discussing marriage."

Jocelyn's jaw dropped. "How can you, after losing Dad? How can you love someone else? How can you get involved in a relationship that is bound to end in pain? Martin could die, too."

"I'm sure he will," said Adelle, "and so will I, but that will happen even if I don't take this opportunity to share my life with him. I feel privileged to have had love not just once, but twice in my life. How many people can say that?"

"Do you love him the way you loved Dad?" Jocelyn asked, picking up a photo of herself wearing a cowboy hat and boots and perched on her father's shoulder.

Adelle shook her head. "No, there is only one first love. That doesn't mean the second is inferior, just different. I must admit that when Martin began calling, I felt a little guilty. But your father is no longer part of my life. I can say that without any bitterness at all. He has gone on to better things, and I am still here. He would be the last person to hold me back from happiness."

Jocelyn framed another photo in strips of self-adhesive paper that resembled fine-grained wood. "Mom, do you think Dad is in heaven?"

"Yes, Jocelyn, but probably not for the reasons you think. He was always a good person by human standards, and I suppose I was, too. When we began having marital problems, we wondered why two good people couldn't agree and make things work. It was then that we learned we had no relationship with God. Your father and I both put our trust in Him to show us how to live this life, and to keep us in the next. I tried to tell you about it before. I guess I didn't do such a good job."

"I think you did. I just wasn't ready. While I was in the hospital, I did the same thing. The chaplain showed me that Jesus was like a bridge to God, the only way we can be forgiven and come to Him. I was too angry before. I just couldn't hear it from you."

Suddenly, she hugged Adelle. "I've hurt you so much. I'm sorry."

Adelle bit back the tears of relief and happiness, knowing Jocelyn would be embarrassed by them. "It's all right, dear," she managed to say. "Really, it is."

Later that evening, Austin stopped in for coffee and dessert.

"You seem preoccupied," said Jocelyn. She had been watching him carefully dissect the layers of pastry in his apple turnover, and his coffee had grown cold long ago.

"I learned something today," he said at last, and turned to look at her. "Gerald Folkert was released from jail. The charges have been dismissed."

"What? How can that be?" she asked. "You showed them the pictures. He was sending them through the mail."

Austin shook his head, staring at his reflection in the cold coffee. "It seems our prosecuting attorney doesn't believe the photographs are pornographic. I was there for the hearing. He said that while Folkert might be guilty of bad taste, the material was not dangerous. He said it's the kind of 'playful nudity'—his words—that can be purchased in any bookstore. Anyway, there's no way to prove Folkert was profiting from the sale of the material without a full-scale investigation." Austin shrugged. "I guess that's the end of it."

"Your heroism wasn't wasted," Jocelyn assured him, slipping her arm around his and holding tightly. "He'll show his hand one day. We know what he is."

Austin smiled. "Always full of hope, aren't you?"

"Always."

When Austin heard about the wedding plans, he was as skeptical as Jocelyn. His conversation with his mother, however, had made him realize that his father had performed admirably under the pressure of their separation. Though Austin was quick to note what he considered faults in his father, he could never remember the man saying an unkind word about his wife, or placing any blame on her for the failed relationship. Their marriage was over, but Martin was not the one who had walked out.

"What assurance do you have that it will work this time?" Austin asked his father as they ate a simple dinner at a cafe.

Martin answered, "None. Nothing concrete, nothing like you want, Austin. Whenever human beings are involved in a plan, there's the opportunity for failure. That's why success is so wonderful. I can only say I love Adelle, and she loves me. I'm thankful God brought her back into my life."

While it was no mystery to Austin that someone would be taken with Adelle, he wondered what she saw in his father, but had the good manners not to ask. Still, he doubted that the two would be compatible. "It's so dangerous," he said.

"Yes, it is," agreed Martin. "It's also dangerous to think you can wait until everything is perfect before making a commitment to another person. Austin, for most of your life, you've tried to make right the greatest wrong that can be done to a young person. In one way or another, you've been trying to correct the terrible mistake your mother and I made. You've worked for security and stability, and that's all right. You want to be dignified and proper. That's all right, too. I'm proud of everything you've accomplished. But you can't create love using some formula. You take love where it comes, but believe me, it doesn't come by chance. It takes work and sacrifice."

"But what if—?"

"Austin, I made a promise to your mother, and I kept that promise," Martin said. Austin tried to adjust to the firmness and conviction in his father's voice. His image of his father was one of a clown, a loser, so to hear him now defending his decisions and feelings was new to Austin. "The end of my first marriage was the greatest sorrow of my life," Martin continued. "But I love Adelle. I will make the same promise to her—to love her until I die. I will keep that promise, just as I kept it to your mother. I hope and pray that Adelle will keep hers. With God's blessing, I believe we can succeed."

"Is it that easy?" Austin asked. "Just make a promise? Feelings change, Dad. Circumstances change. Look at Adelle. She's nothing like my mother. Can you love the same person at forty that you loved at twenty? When you and Adelle are retired, will your interests be the same? Will you even like each other, let alone love each other?"

"A man makes a choice," said Martin. "The thing I've learned is that the choice is just the beginning. I loved your mother long after she was gone, but she made her own decision. I wasn't totally innocent of blame. I didn't plan for change. I didn't think about the fact that she would need more than I could give her in the way of friendships and diversions. To put it simply, I took her for granted for a long time. By the time I came to my senses, she didn't want to try anymore."

Martin swallowed the last of his chocolate milk and dunked a french fry in ketchup. He chewed it thoughtfully, then said, "Maybe the biggest thing of all, Austin, is that Adelle and I share a common faith. Both of us want to have our lives under the direction of God. That isn't the only thing that has to happen in a good relationship, but it's the best place to begin."

Austin's interest quickened. "I've been thinking along those very lines. First, people should build a spiritual foundation for their lives, then add the rest. But—" he paused, hardly believing that he was about to ask his father for advice. Still, the man seemed to know something Austin did not. There could be no better time. "How do you begin?"

Martin tossed a crumpled napkin on the table. "First,

you confess to God that you have nothing of any value to offer Him. Can you do that?"

Austin was slow to answer, knowing how he had taken pride in his possessions and his effective life. At last, he understood they were empty in the light of eternity.

"Yes, I can do that."

"Then the rest is easy," said Martin, "because God has done it all."

❧

Adelle gave a party. While their many mutual friends listened with obvious pleasure, Martin and Adelle made the formal announcement of their intention to marry. Austin and Jocelyn stood side by side, looking at their parents, not at each other. Their mixed feelings of envy and apprehension were carefully hidden as they clapped along with the other guests. Both were wondering how it could ever work.

"Austin, I'm moving back to my house as soon as the weather warms up," Jocelyn said as he was preparing to go.

"I would have argued about that a while ago," replied Austin, "but I don't want to deny you the satisfaction of completing the course you started. Your Aunt Bebe must have known you pretty well. Her legacy seems to be the string that holds your life together."

"In more ways than one," agreed Jocelyn. "I miss the old place. I miss my work. My mom's being patient with me, but I know it's getting on her nerves to have me up at daylight and reading junk mail all day. I don't want to lose momentum. I think the business is just starting to work for me."

"Well, I'm doing my part," said Austin. "I have your mail in the car. I'll bring it in."

"I'll walk out with you." She took Austin's hand and walked down the steps, then watched for the reflection of the moon in the puddles on the sidewalk to avoid stepping in the water.

"I can't believe it's spring already," she said.

"Love is in the air," Austin responded, turning to face her as they came to the car. "We could have a double wedding with our parents, if you're ready to say yes."

"Oh, I couldn't do that," said Jocelyn with feigned intensity. "You know how particular I am. I would need at least a year to plan and prepare."

Austin smiled. "Right. I forgot. You never do anything on the spur of the moment." He continued to hold her hand a moment, then said, "Even though I want to hear you say yes, I'm happy that you are taking your time and not rushing into marriage. I've always thought I could control my life. But after all that's happened, I know I can't. I do know that I love you very much. I am more certain of it every day."

As his lips met hers in a brief good-night kiss, Jocelyn almost agreed to marry him. What was she waiting for? He loved her, wanted her, and she knew he would always be faithful. Now it seemed they were on the same spiritual path that would make them completely one. Could anything yet be lacking?

He held her for a moment and her thoughts wandered wildly over the events of their few short months together. Whatever it was she was still seeking, she realized, must come from herself, not from Austin, and so far, she could not identify it.

nine

April

"It's the most romantic thing I've ever heard of in my life," said Jocelyn. She read the letter that Greta had handed her one more time. "He wants to marry you. What are you going to say?"

"What do you think?" asked Greta. She sat at her kitchen table, massaging oil into her cuticles. "I would be absolutely crazy to turn him down."

"But you haven't actually seen Randolph in person, in the flesh, since the day you met him, right? What if these letters were made up by some friend of his? You know, like Cyrano de Bergerac or something."

"They could be," said Greta. "You helped me write some to him. I suppose he could do the same thing."

"But then you don't really know what he's like, do you?"

Greta shrugged, and examined her nails. "He signed the letters. Even if he didn't write the words himself, they tell me how he feels, and that's more important than what a person says. Wait until you see him. He's gorgeous. He has his own salon in a little town of about twelve thousand people, in Wisconsin. He says all kinds of people come to him, old ladies who want frizzy perms, and kids who want half their head shaved, and everything in between. I'll work with him after we're married."

"Are you sure he isn't just marrying you so he can have cheap help?" Jocelyn asked.

"Believe me," Greta said testily, "he doesn't have to get married to get a woman to come and live with him. Anyway, don't you think he really could love me just for myself?"

Jocelyn threw her arms around her friend. "Greta, I never meant that you aren't the greatest catch in the world. You're beautiful and talented, and any guy would be lucky to have you. I'm just afraid—I don't know of what. Maybe he's got some hidden agenda."

Greta nodded. "I think about that. When I met Randolph at the cosmetology convention a year and a half ago, I knew it was not the kind of situation where I expected to find a serious relationship. I mean, it was one hundred women for every man, and a lot of those men didn't actually count, if you know what I mean. Randolph was like the only star in the sky. When he introduced himself to me, I looked around to see who he was talking to."

"Don't sell yourself short. You are very pretty."

"Yeah, yeah," Greta said, waving one long, slim hand in the air. "Anyway, he said he noticed me because I'm tall, and he likes tall girls, though he's only about an inch taller than I am. He was just. . .nice. I can't explain it, but we just clicked."

"And now he's proposing, and you're going to say yes."

A slow smile spread across Greta's face. She pushed clenched fists up to her chin, and shivered slightly. "Yes. Yes. Yes. I am really going to say yes!"

"The letter says he'll be here the day after tomorrow," said Jocelyn. "He's flying in. Are you going to meet him at the airport?"

Greta nodded. "I already called him. I didn't tell him I accepted his proposal, but I said I would meet him. I think he knows. I wouldn't have encouraged him to fly over here if I weren't going to say yes."

"Am I going to get to meet him?"

"Jocelyn! Of course! I want you and Austin to go with me to the airport. Just because I've made up my mind, it doesn't mean I don't need support. After all, you helped me write letters to Randolph, and Austin brought his letters to me. You're practically cupids yourselves."

Jocelyn walked home, reveling in the crisp, fresh air, and the sight of new green in the woods. Echoing through the trees was the sound of heavy equipment from the new subdivision being built almost directly behind her home. Soon, she knew, she would be surrounded by new homes. Her ugly duckling house would never grow into a swan, however. The neighbors would grow to hate her and complain to the township building inspector about the rotting porch, her unmowed grass, and unpainted siding.

Money was the key. If only she could put a few thousand dollars into the place, she knew she could make it acceptable, at least on the outside. As she walked along the road bordered by ditches where cattails sprouted and sumac was greening, she wondered how long it would be until it was all gone, with every piece of land groomed and sanitized, or covered by concrete or blacktop. She knew she could not reasonably deny anyone the opportunity to build a home here. Aunt Bebe's parents had built nearly a century ago, and now Jocelyn looked at the fruits of their labor coming into view—a faded, rattletrap house that looked like it would crash with the first strong wind.

Along with her home, Jocelyn's dreams were threatening to tumble down. She continued to make just enough money to keep going, but never enough to get ahead. She marveled now when she remembered how, in her college days, she had eaten at fast-food restaurants, attended concerts, bought shoes and makeup and books. Back then, the allowance she received from her father's inheritance was more than she needed for her conservative lifestyle, and a part-time job provided money to spend on friends.

Adelle had tried to persuade Jocelyn to continue accepting her allowance after she moved into Aunt Bebe's house and began her work as a contestant, but she refused.

"If I can't make it on my own, I'll come crawling back," she had told her mother. "Don't worry. You can be the first to gloat." She now realized how unkind she had been, and had asked her mother's forgiveness for that and other specific occasions when she had been rude. However, she still refused the money. *As soon as I turn twenty-one, the allowance would no longer be available anyway, so no sense worrying about that,* Jocelyn thought as she walked up the creaking steps. It was probably a good thing. She had grown to love the old place with its memories and eccentricities, and now its association with Austin. She did not want to leave, and certainly did not want to sell.

As she glanced back along the quiet road, however, Jocelyn realized how alone she was. The neighbors on both sides of her home had sold their property within the last year. Mr. Vanderlaan, she remembered, had decided to sell after several incidents of vandalism had left him too frightened to stay alone in his house. Another neighbor had decided to sell when his well failed, and he learned how much his assessment for city water would be. Police had wondered whether that too had been vandalism, according to a story in the local paper, but nothing could be proven.

Her one concession to Austin's haranguing about safety was to have a telephone installed. It was ringing as she entered the living room.

"Hello, Jocelyn, it's Austin." She heard the familiar voice, which never failed to resonate on some deep level within her. "I want to warn you that Gerald Folkert is back at his house. I saw him there this morning when I went by."

Jocelyn glanced out the side window and through the still-bare branches and saw Gerald's truck in his driveway.

Austin continued, "I don't think he has any quarrel with you, but just keep an eye out for him, all right? He isn't the kind of person who would confront anyone directly. He's just slimy. I don't trust him at all."

Jocelyn told Austin about Greta's proposal. "Randolph's flying in the day after tomorrow. Can you come with us to the airport? Greta wants you along."

"I think I can arrange it," he said. "He sounds like someone I should meet. His technique worked when mine failed."

"Do you think it's a good idea?" asked Jocelyn. "They know nothing about each other except what they've read in their letters and talked about on the phone. I mean, he's never seen her without her makeup. She's never cooked for him. She's never seen him lose his temper."

"Do you want to know what I think?" asked Austin. "I think people don't know each other when they get married, no matter how long they've hung around each other. When you get married, you make a promise that, no matter what you discover, you will work through it somehow. Some people keep their promises. Some don't."

"Well, no one deserves happiness more than Greta. She's been such a good friend to me. I hate the thought of her moving off to Wisconsin."

"It's not the other side of the world," said Austin. "You don't even need a passport to get to Wisconsin. You can go and visit."

"Well, let's get a firsthand look at Randolph. Then we can make plans." As Jocelyn hung up the phone, she noticed Gerald Folkert's truck coming down the road, slowing as it passed her house, then speeding up again. She watched until it passed over the hill, then exhaled.

❧

Greta bounced nervously in the back seat of Austin's car.

"We'll never get there on time," she said. "Look! There are emergency lights up there. There's been an accident. We'll be stuck on the expressway for hours."

Austin quickly maneuvered toward the exit and got off the expressway.

"You can't get to the airport this way," said Greta.

"Trust me," replied Austin. "I know every residential street between here and Hastings. We'll get there."

By winding through subdivisions and business parks, they finally arrived at the Kent County airport. Greta and Jocelyn ran in to check on incoming flights while Austin parked the car.

"He's late!" Greta said jubilantly when Austin found them. "The plane should be here in about fifteen minutes."

"Do you think you'll remember what he looks like?" Austin asked. "A year and a half—a lot can change."

"The question is, will he remember me?" Greta mused.

Silently, they walked along the concourse to the runway gate, and sat and waited.

Anxiously, Greta tried to look farther and farther down the ramps where passengers were deplaning. At last, her face brightened, and Austin and Jocelyn caught sight of a slightly built man in a black designer shirt and white, pleated pants. His long, blond hair was shorter around his face, and curly above his collar. His dark sandals were of the same material as his bag, and when he took off his sunglasses, they could see, even from a distance, his brilliant blue eyes.

"It's him," Greta breathed, and took a step forward.

Randolph also was searching, and he suddenly spotted Greta. He waved the sunglasses above his head in salute, and broke into a grin. Tentatively, the two approached one another, then met a short distance away from Austin and Jocelyn.

"What's he saying?" Jocelyn whispered.

Austin shook his head. "I can't tell. Probably something to break the ice, like, 'Let's get married this afternoon.' "

In a moment, Greta and Randolph returned. After the introductions, the two couples went to the airport coffee shop.

"Do you need a place to stay while you're in town?" Austin asked as they waited for coffee. "I have an extra room. You're completely welcome."

Randolph looked cautiously at Greta. "I had assumed I would get a motel room," he said. "I don't mind saying the offer interests me. I hate motels."

"You can trust him," said Greta. "He's a mailman."

Austin delivered Greta and Randolph to her home. "I know you two will have plenty to talk about," said Austin, taking a key off his key ring. "Here's the key to the house. I take it Greta will be bringing you over later?"

Randolph nodded. "It may be late."

"Well, I'm only your host, not your chaperone," said Austin. "I go to bed early, so I'll just leave a light on in your room."

As Austin drove Jocelyn home, she said, "I can't believe you did that. You are not the same man you were a few months ago. You just invited a total stranger into your home, gave him your key, and you don't even plan to stay up to explain the house rules. What if he uses the bath towel as a floor mat?"

"Was I that bad?" Austin asked. "You make me sound like an old-maid aunt."

"Well, it's just such a change from the man who wouldn't give me my mail without seeing some identification. I think the change is wonderful."

"He seems normal enough," said Austin. "I don't know what I was expecting."

"Greta let me read some of his letters. They were very newsy—you know, relaxed and chatty, not romantic. But then she didn't show me all of them. He'll be here for three days."

"I feel like we aren't saying what we want to say," Austin replied.

Jocelyn cast a sideways glance. "You mean questions like, 'Are there men in black suits with names like Mickey and Vinny who loaned him money to start the salon and now are parked in front every day when he arrives?' "

Austin laughed. "Yes! That's the kind of question I really want to ask, but I'm too polite. I want to ask, 'What about that string of unsolved homicides in Wisconsin? Do you know anything about that?' "

"Oh, Austin! Don't even say it!" Jocelyn cried. "I've been polite, too, but I really am worried. Could he have some devious plan we haven't imagined?"

"He could, but we'll have to trust Greta, won't we?"

Jocelyn grew quiet, then said, "Remember what you told me, about not really knowing someone when you get married? Do you think you could be faithful to someone who turned out to be a monster? What if some girl married Gerald Folkert, thinking he was just a photographer, then found out what he does. Should she stay with him?"

"Or what if Greta finds out Randolph is only looking for a business partner, not a love relationship?" Austin asked.

Jocelyn nodded. "What can you do?"

"I don't know," Austin said, and he knew that he and Jocelyn both were thinking of each other even as they discussed their friends. What if, after all his pleading and planning, Austin one day found that Jocelyn's eccentricities were no longer endearing, but irritating? What if, instead of depending on his strength, she came to loathe his inflexibility?

"You said it depends on keeping your promise," said Jocelyn. "Is that all? Do you just suffer through it?"

Austin hesitated. "Maybe that's where spiritual values make the difference. If God is interested in our lives and wants to have a relationship with us, wouldn't He have some plan for getting through the hard times?"

When I am afraid, I will trust in you.

Aunt Bebe's back door verse came to Jocelyn's mind. There would be no need to trust if all the answers could be known in advance. The Bible would not include a verse like that if times of fear were not part of the normal existence. But it implied that God had the answer.

Jocelyn nodded. "We have so much to learn," she said.

"You mean, about each other?"

"About this whole new life."

They had been sitting in Jocelyn's driveway as they talked, enjoying the quiet spring evening and the still-early sunset. As the shadows became long across Greenwood Road, however, Jocelyn once again saw Gerald Folkert's truck approaching her house. This time, the truck slowed to a stop behind Austin's parked car. She saw Gerald stare at them briefly, then drive toward the highway.

"He's scaring me," said Jocelyn softly, watching the truck vanish in the distance.

"I think that's what he means to do," replied Austin. "As I said, I don't think he would hurt you. He's a weak person who preys on the weak. He's learned by now that he can't intimidate you."

Jocelyn turned to Austin, blinking. "He can't? I think he just did."

"You're alarmed, not intimidated. Big difference. I'll stay, if you want me to."

Jocelyn shook her head. "I promised myself I would work this evening since I took the afternoon off to be with Greta. You're right, of course. He doesn't have the guts to actually do any damage."

"I'll be at home," Austin said. "Call if you need me." He waved as he pulled away from the house, and he didn't notice that Gerald's truck was concealed in the shady drive of an abandoned barn across the road from Jocelyn's house.

When Folkert saw Austin's car go by, he immediately headed toward Jocelyn's house. She saw him pull into the driveway, and tried to think what she should do. She stood in the middle of the living room as he walked toward the front door. Her heart raced as she heard his demanding knock.

Jocelyn waited a moment, then opened the door partway. "Yes?"

"Hello, Jocelyn," said Gerald in a voice that was too friendly. "Say, I noticed your boyfriend here a little while ago. Sorry I missed him. I've been wanting to tell him something."

"Write a letter," responded Jocelyn without a smile. "He'll deliver it to himself tomorrow."

Folkert laughed. "Pretty cute. That's what I like about you. Sorry we couldn't do any business, but tell your boyfriend he can expect a message from me any day."

"Why are you telling me?" Jocelyn demanded. "Why don't you speak to him yourself? Or are you afraid of him?"

"You bet I'm afraid of him," Folkert said, leaning closer to Jocelyn's face. She pulled away from the door, keeping her foot against the back of it as he pushed on the front. "He beat me up, stole my property, tried to have me thrown in jail. Jail's not a nice place to be. Maybe he'll find that out." He turned and went halfway down the steps, then called back over his shoulder, "Just tell him!"

ten

May

Nodding tulips along the border of her home failed to brighten Jocelyn's mood. The ancient crabapple tree filled the air with its intoxicating fragrance, and clouds of migrating birds lent their color to the bunches of pale blossoms, but Jocelyn's mind was elsewhere.

Among the piles of contest materials also lay three months' worth of unpaid bills for electricity, a notice of the lapse of her car insurance, and a notice from the township that she was being assessed $6,543 for a new water line that was to be installed to serve the new developments in the area. An easy payment plan would be arranged, the notice stated. She learned the payments amounted to only twice the amount of her average weekly earnings during the past two months. The longer hours of daylight should have cheered her, but they seemed to only lengthen her hopeless days.

On Easter Sunday, Jocelyn had made a promise to God which she had revealed to no one else. It was that she would trust Him completely to direct her life, and not question or try to manipulate that direction. Would He now take from her the things that had been the driving force in her life? She wondered.

Austin interrupted her reverie, arriving with a pizza and

several sharp pencils. He had learned that Jocelyn had never completed her income tax return, although she had begun working on the forms shortly after she had moved back from her stay at her mother's house.

"I know it's all there in the fine print," said Jocelyn. "I just don't seem to have the patience to read it. It isn't like when I was in school. The textbooks were interesting. There was information about real things. This is just words. It's so boring."

Austin sat at the kitchen table, punching numbers on a pocket calculator in one hand while holding a slice of pizza in the other. Jocelyn looked on anxiously, answering questions or digging through her bag of receipts, bank statements, and check stubs.

At last, Austin sat back and sighed. "You did pretty well for a first year in business. You apparently made $5,327.13. You had only $867.29 in expenses. It looks like you will have to pay only a couple of hundred dollars, plus the late fees."

Jocelyn let her head sink down to the table. "That's the last straw," she muttered, hoping Austin would think she was joking. She did not want him to see her tears.

Austin said nothing. He continued to add the final details to the tax return, then bundled all of Jocelyn's receipts back into the bag.

"Keep this somewhere safe," he said. "The IRS keeps a pretty sharp eye on new businesses. They might have questions."

Jocelyn got up from the old wooden chair—the same one where she had often sat as a child eating Aunt Bebe's homemade soup. She went to the window and looked out toward the back of the property, now bordered with asparagus and chives gone wild, and dozens of sapling willow trees, their leaves still yellow-green.

"Aunt Bebe supported herself on a little mail-order business selling dried herbs and spice mixes," said Jocelyn. "That pantry you see, now so empty, was her storeroom. If you walk in there, you can still smell the aroma. She started with nothing, and built a small business that provided a good living for her in her old age." She turned to Austin, now unable to control the tears. "Did I want so much, just to do what she did? Just to live my life without being a burden to anyone? Why won't God let me do it?"

"It isn't like that," Austin said. "You made a profit. Most businesses fail in the first two years. You started with no capital. You started with nothing in reserve."

She shook her head and turned back to the window. "It could have worked. God is just saying no. I told Him I would pay attention and do what He wanted me to do. I'm just disappointed that this is what He wants from me—to give up my house and work and start over, or go back to being a dental technician."

Austin went to her and gently turned her face toward his own. "Have you considered that maybe this is His way of telling you that you should marry me? I haven't said anything about it for weeks, waiting for you to decide what you were going to do. Now it seems pretty obvious you can't continue to live as you have. Marry me, Jocelyn. Not because you need me, or because I have everything all figured out. Marry me because I love you. Marry me because you love me."

A cardinal perched in the pine tree across the driveway and began to sing. In a moment, a female appeared, and the two dropped down into the gravel drive to peck at the stones and search for seeds.

"Yes," she said quietly. "I'll marry you. I've loved you almost since the day I met you, and I know you love me. It's time. I don't know why I've waited so long."

Austin held her tight, kissing her with a new passion that left her breathless, still teary-eyed, and a little confused.

"Let's call your mother," suggested Austin. "She and Dad are working out the details of their wedding right now. It's the perfect time."

"The telephone was shut off two weeks ago," said Jocelyn. "Anyway, we should go in person."

"Yes! Better idea!" exclaimed Austin, grabbing his pencils and calculator. Then he kissed Jocelyn again. Jocelyn wondered if it was to keep her from thinking too much about her decision.

Martin and Adelle suggested a double wedding, but Jocelyn refused.

"You deserve the spotlight all to yourselves," she said.

"And so do you," said Martin. He looked first at Adelle, then at Austin and Jocelyn. "I'm so happy. I never expected to be this happy in my life. What more could anyone ask?" Suddenly his facial expression changed, and he took out a notepad and an old pencil stub that had been sharpened with a knife. He began scribbling.

"Inspiration," Adelle said to Jocelyn. "He has an idea and doesn't want to lose it."

"It's a card game," Martin explained, not looking up, "called What's Better Than. . . ? You draw a card, and if what you get is better than what's in your hand, you keep it or give it away. And there are points. Finding a twenty dollar bill, for instance, might be worth six points; getting married could be ten points. And there would have to be 'worse than' cards to mix in—funny situations—worse than a bee sting? Depends on where it is. . ."

He was oblivious to their laughter, and Jocelyn's spirits lifted as they shared their moment of joy. She had been right to trust. She had always believed love would catch her unaware, lift her up, and carry her away. It was no less sweet because it had gradually worked its way into her life through cracks she had left unguarded.

When Austin drove Jocelyn home, he looked to make sure there was no one in the house.

"If Folkert shows up, call the police," he said. "Tell them he's stalking you."

"I can't," she said. "There's—"

"No phone," Austin finished. "I'm going to bring you my cellular tomorrow." She started to protest, and he put his fingers on her lips. "Aren't we beyond all that yet? I don't know what that man is up to, but I want to know you have some way to get help if he decides to do anything strange. Wouldn't you rather go up and stay with Greta?"

"Didn't you know?" asked Jocelyn. "She left this morning for Wisconsin. She's spending the weekend with Randolph's family."

"I forgot. It sounds like they're proceeding with caution, even though they've made the decision to get married. Did they set the date?"

Jocelyn nodded. "They're planning for the end of July, a

small wedding in Chicago. That way, everyone has to travel, and no one goes too far. There's another big convention then, and they want to work it into their honeymoon."

"And you thought I was too practical," teased Austin. "How would it be if we get married on a Monday holiday so I don't have to miss work?" He took a deep breath and grinned at her. "Married! I've been wanting to hear you say yes for so long, but I can hardly believe it. Jocelyn, I love you."

"Even though I'm poor?" she asked, taking his hands in hers.

"You're not poor," he said. "You're flat broke. We'll have to talk about your options—whether you want to sell the property here, where you'll live until we're married." He saw her expression change, and her smile begin to fade, and quickly added, "Tomorrow will be soon enough for all that. There's plenty of time for decisions." He offered a quick good-night kiss and went out the door.

Jocelyn sat down on the couch, but had no heart to begin looking at the piles of contest offers that had come in this morning's mail. The day had been taken up with preparation for Austin to finish the income tax return, and now Jocelyn was faced with the prospect of doing extra work each day to catch up, all for the privilege of paying to the government money she did not have. It was too discouraging. She decided to take a walk, enjoy the evening, and start fresh in the morning.

Instead of walking on the road, Jocelyn took a path through the woods toward the new subdivision. The machinery was quiet now, and she wanted to get a look at how the new neighbors would be living. The cleared area was surprisingly close to Jocelyn's home. During the winter, she guessed, she might even be able to see homes that were on higher elevations.

Some of the streets were already blacktopped, and two homes were under construction, though the preliminary development work was far from over. Jocelyn walked along the smooth, new street for a short way, but when she saw a large burgundy sedan pull into the entrance, she ducked back into the woods. She felt guilty, unsure whether she had a right to be there. She stood in the shadows and waited to see if the car would go on through the development. It was probably neighbors, who, like herself, were curious to see how the place was shaping up.

The dark sedan stopped near the path where Jocelyn had come through the woods, and two men got out. One of them was Gerald Folkert.

"No, the property is adjacent," said the driver as they went around to the front of the car and pointed toward the woods. "You should have had it taken care of long ago. As it is, it's hardly any advantage to us now, what with this project already approved. A few more acres last summer would have made a difference. Now—"

"It will be happening soon," said Gerald, "and now that Vanderlaan and the others are out of the way, you could do about anything you wanted here."

Jocelyn listened, but the words made no sense. They began to talk about zoning ordinances, and then got back into the car and drove away. She turned back into the woods, found the path, and was at her back door in fifteen minutes. But for some reason, she did not feel safe.

eleven

June

Jocelyn stood beside the mailbox, waiting for Austin to arrive. She had been working since 5:00 A.M., but had not yet caught up with the overload of mail. For the first time since becoming a professional contestant, she wished no mail would arrive.

When Austin finally pulled up next to the mailbox, Jocelyn knew immediately that something was wrong. "There's trouble," she stated, as he began handing her the mail.

He nodded. "Just a work thing," he said. "I'll stop over this afternoon and tell you about it. Don't worry. It will work out."

"I can't believe you said that," said Jocelyn. "It seems we've completely reversed roles."

All day she worked, quickly eliminating those pieces which held little promise, then carefully reading each item that fit her business principals and plan. She forced herself not to think about the fact that in a matter of weeks, it might all be over. Austin's mention of selling the property as one method to get her out of financial constraints kept coming to her mind, and she kept forcing it away. She thought of the herbs gone wild along the western edge of the yard, a half-acre that Aunt Bebe had cultivated and harvested as part of her business. *How Austin would love to resurrect it,* Jocelyn thought. She must remember to tell him about it. But why should she, if the land had to be sold?

When Jocelyn heard Austin's car in the driveway, she assumed he must have come directly from the station. Sure enough, he was still in his uniform. That made her even more worried. She met him at the door with a hug and brought him ice water with a slice of lemon. They sat side by side on the couch.

"I've been laid off," said Austin. "The new postmaster who started three weeks ago has an eye to greater efficiency, and I have the least seniority. One other full-time person was cut, and a part-timer was transferred."

"But I thought the post office was next to being in the military," Jocelyn said. "Postal workers never lose their jobs. They're like teachers. Once they're in, they're in for life."

"Well, it isn't quite like that. I can still work, if I want to go back to part-time status and take a pay cut and wait for another full-time opening somewhere. It might not even be here in town."

"How much of a pay cut?" asked Jocelyn.

"About 30 percent, and almost no benefits."

"But at least you would still be working. How much money do you make, anyway? Seventy percent of what you make is probably about 200 percent of what I make."

"It isn't just the money," he replied. "There's no guarantee that a full-time job will materialize, and if it does, it may be in another city."

"But we could go anywhere," said Jocelyn, idly leafing through a stack of envelopes. The return address on one of them caught her eye, and as Austin continued to talk about the uncertainties he now faced, she opened it and quickly scanned the single-page letter inside, thinking it was a bill for the subscription to her contestant's magazine.

"I know I already paid this," she mumbled. "I sent it in January."

"What? Are you listening, Jocelyn? This could change everything."

Her face wrinkled in a scowl, and she did not answer. Instead, she began reading the letter out loud.

"—This year's winner of the *Prizewinner's Bulletin*—benefitting from increased membership. Austin, I've won something I didn't enter. I don't understand this." Once again, she started at the top of the letter, and carefully read each sentence as Austin waited impatiently for her attention. He wanted to talk about the future, and she was still dabbling in prizewinning.

At last, Jocelyn looked at the man she intended to marry, and said, "I'm rich." She held up a check in one hand, and the letter in the other. "I'm rich, and I had nothing to do with it. All my hard work for a year comes down to the luck of the draw."

Like a television rerun, Jocelyn remembered herself on hands and knees on the living room floor, shuffling through the mail. "If You control everything, You control these contests," she had prayed that day. What she had not considered was God's sense of timing.

Austin sighed. "What is it this time? A whopping hundred dollar prize? Maybe you can have the telephone put back in."

"I won $247,000," said Jocelyn quietly.

Austin took the check and looked at it. "Isn't this

$247?" he asked, not believing that the location of the decimal was correct. "What is this? Is it the lottery?"

"I told you I never gamble, and I meant it. In January, I got a notice that my subscription to *Prizewinner's Bulletin* had run out. I paid for another year. According to the letter, they put the names of all subscribers in a barrel and draw one as the winner of a cash prize given by the publisher of the magazine. I'm it. Don't you see the irony?" She stared at Austin. "This is. . ." She held up her hands, slowly shaking her head, and said nothing.

Austin once again looked at the check, running his finger along the row of numbers. He read the letter. It was as Jocelyn had said.

Austin stared at her. "You are rich," he said. "Even figuring taxes on the winnings, you can easily live on the interest from this money, if you don't care whether you upgrade your lifestyle. In fact, you can do just about anything you want to do."

There was no joy in Austin's voice, and Jocelyn immediately understood that everything had changed. She got up from the couch and walked across the room.

"Then we could get married right away," Jocelyn said. "We don't have to worry about money anymore. You don't even need to work. You can work here! I was going to show you the herb garden tonight, Austin. Wait until you see it. It's just waiting for someone like you to take a hand—"

"Jocelyn, you're babbling again."

When she turned to him, there were tears in her eyes. "This doesn't make any difference," she said, clutching the check in her fist. "We are still the same."

"Are we?" Austin asked. "I don't think so."

"But I need you to manage things for me. I don't know what to do with money. I've never had any of my own."

Austin smiled gently. "Funny, a couple of months ago, the one thing keeping you from marrying me was that you didn't want to feel the relationship was based on need. Don't you see I feel the same way? It's my turn now, Jocelyn. I have to think about where I'm going in my life, and just what you and I want from each other. I want to be sure."

Jocelyn nodded, fighting back the tears. Austin went out the front door without a good-bye, and when she knew he had driven away, she sat on the couch and sobbed, her tears dampening the check she still held tightly.

❧

Jocelyn and Austin stood side by side in front of friends and family members as their parents exchanged wedding vows. They did not look at each other. The familiar words—love, honor, cherish until death—fell like hammer blows on their hearts. They had argued at length for the first time four days ago when they tried to discuss whether they should go ahead with wedding plans. Now, the obvious happiness and contentment of their parents taunted them.

The ceremony was short and simple, and was held in the chapel at the botanical gardens. The Van Dorans greeted guests in the banquet room. The bridesmaid and best man stood on opposite sides of the room and tried to keep from answering personal questions.

Jocelyn kissed her mother as Adelle got into Martin's car.

"Be happy, Mom," she said.

"Jocelyn, I can hardly bear to leave you," said Adelle. "I

wish you would work this out with Austin. Surely you two are far too sensible to let money, or the absence of it, come between you."

"It's more than that. He's only giving me what I gave him. I was afraid of losing my independence. He is, too."

Adelle shook her head. "You've both missed the point. This whole thing—everything that's happened to you—should show you that it's God who is really in control. Why can't you both give in at the same time?"

"Don't think about us," Jocelyn said, putting on a smile. "You and Martin enjoy your trip. I did have the phone put back in. You can call me if you want."

"Martin will be busy visiting the toy manufacturers, and I'm going to see the city. There won't be a lot of time."

"Some honeymoon," Jocelyn chided. "You won't even see each other."

"We have all the rest of our lives," said Adelle.

So do I, Jocelyn thought as she waved at the departing vehicle, *and it looks like I'll have it all to myself.*

When the gifts were packed and the caterers had cleared the room, Jocelyn got into her old Lincoln to drive the short distance home. She was tired and sad and the last person in the world she wanted to see was the one sitting in his truck in her driveway.

Jocelyn walked up to the truck and knocked sharply on the window. "What are you doing here?" she demanded through the glass.

Gerald rolled down the window. "Nice dress," he said. "I heard about the wedding. I figured you'd be back soon, so I decided to wait. Not your wedding, though, was it?"

"What do you want?" she asked. "I'm sick and tired of

you hanging around here. I can't make you move out of the neighborhood, but you had sure better stay away from my house." Jocelyn felt herself beginning to shake, and she pressed her lips firmly together, glared at Gerald, and tried to control her breathing.

"It's not me who should be moving," said Gerald. "It's you. This old house—it's unsafe, you know. It could even burn up or something like that. Oh, and that message for your boyfriend I mentioned? I think it's being delivered this evening."

"Get away from here before I call the police," warned Jocelyn.

"Call," said Gerald. "There's nothing you can pin on me. I'm just an honest businessman, not unlike yourself. Speaking of which," he continued, pulling a card from his shirt pocket, "I know someone who might take this swamp off your hands." He waved the card in the direction of the woods around Jocelyn's home, then handed it to her. "It's a liability to you, and believe me, it could get a lot worse. Take my advice. Get rid of this place. I know you need the cash, and so does your boyfriend."

Gerald pulled his truck across the yard and onto the road and drove away. Jocelyn ran to the house and called Austin. The phone rang eight times before he finally answered, and his voice sounded slurred.

"Austin! What's wrong?"

"Couple of guys jumped me," he said with obvious effort. "I came home, they were waiting for me, landed some good punches before I could get away. They drove off before I could get a license number."

"It's Gerald!" Jocelyn said. "I'm sure of it. He told me

to tell you to expect a message. He was just here when I got home and said you'd get the message tonight. I'm coming right now." She hung up and raced to her car.

When she arrived at Austin's home, she could see the broken shrubbery near the door where the fight had happened. On the quiet street, no one was about. No children were playing or riding bicycles, no men were cutting the grass, no women were digging in the flower beds. The attackers must have watched for several days to make sure they would catch Austin at home at a time when his neighbors would be indoors. *How long had Gerald been planning this?* Jocelyn wondered. How could they prove it was his idea?

Austin had locked the door. Jocelyn pounded until he finally came and opened it slightly. He held an ice pack to his face, but Jocelyn could see the split skin below his eye, which was already beginning to swell. His bottom lip, too, was nearly double its normal size.

"Did you call the police?" Jocelyn asked, stepping inside.

"Yes, though I doubt it will do a lot of good," said Austin. "Especially after that fiasco in which Gerald came out looking like an upstanding citizen. They are likely to think I'm trying to hassle him instead of the other way around."

Jocelyn waited with Austin until a patrolman arrived to take Austin's complaint. He described the men who had attacked him, and told the officers how he had defended himself using the "shepherd's crook" which had held a hanging basket near his door.

"I just pulled it up and started swinging," said Austin.

"They didn't do much damage to me, except for the first couple of punches. If they had intended any serious harm, I think they would have had weapons."

"Do you think they intended to rob you?" questioned the officer.

Austin shook his head and looked at Jocelyn. "We had a run-in with one of Jocelyn's neighbors a while back. I think this was a payback, but I doubt you can connect him to this attack."

The officer noted Gerald's name, and then Austin described the vehicle in which the attackers had fled. Jocelyn suddenly shouted, "Hey, that's the car I saw at the new development! Gerald was with the driver."

When the interview was over, Jocelyn drove Austin to the walk-in clinic. He insisted he was not hurt badly enough to go to the hospital, but promised that if he felt worse the next day he would go.

As he got out of the Lincoln, Austin sighed and said, "Well, at least I don't have to work tomorrow. I guess it's a good thing I'm suddenly underemployed."

"I'll come over in the morning," Jocelyn said, "just to check on you."

"There's no need—" he started, but Jocelyn interrupted him.

"I'm coming over. That's the end of it."

When Jocelyn arrived the next day, she was greeted by a stranger, someone who might have been Austin's brother.

"Hello," she said tentatively, "is Austin—" Then she realized it was Austin, without his beard. "You shaved!" she cried. The smooth, light skin, combined with the swollen eye, bruised cheek, and enlarged bottom lip had made him unrecognizable at first glance.

He smiled gingerly, obviously in some pain. "This is the real me. Come on in." Then, pointing to his swollen eye, he said, "This isn't the worst of it."

twelve

July

"Folkert has filed a civil suit against me," said Austin. "He's claiming physical harm, mental stress, damage to his reputation, and a few other minor complaints. He's asking for $500,000 in damages, and says he'll settle out of court for $300,000. I just learned about it this morning. I think the episode last night was just to reinforce the idea that he means business."

"But what business?" Jocelyn asked. "What does it have to do with me? What was he doing out at the development? He was talking with that man about zoning ordinances and property lines. They mentioned Mr. Vanderlaan."

Austin lay down on the couch and slowly lowered his head onto a large pillow. "I can understand the suit, and the beating," he said. "Folkert's just angry, and is trying to get back at me. But why would he still be after you? He certainly can't think you'll change your mind and model for his sleazy photos."

"Mr. Vanderlaan," Jocelyn repeated. "I wonder if Folkert was behind the vandalism that drove him out of the neighborhood."

"It's possible. Maybe Mr. Vanderlaan also caught on to Folkert's business."

"Well, forget about him for now," said Jocelyn. "How

are the wounds this morning?"

"I'll be all right," assured Austin. "I don't think I'll be very pretty for Greta's wedding, though. I'm glad those hoodlums had the decency to wait until after our parents' wedding to smash my face in. I decided to shave to make these cuts more accessible for treatment."

"I like it," said Jocelyn. "There was always something wrong with that beard. Why did you grow it in the first place?"

"Look at me," he said, and turned his face full to hers. "Imagine me with glasses."

Jocelyn's face brightened. "Your dad! You look just like your dad! Even with the swelling, I can see it."

"I suppose it was childish, but I didn't want to accept that I was like him in any way. We've pretty well come to terms, like you and your mother, I suppose."

Jocelyn had no reply. It seemed everyone was at peace now, except her and Austin. She was sure Austin would not consider marriage now.

Austin called the sheriff's department and explained the possible connection between Folkert and the vandalism on Greenwood Road.

"They're sending a detective over," said Austin as he hung up. "Maybe they can find the connection between Folkert and that mystery man you saw at the development."

"That might take a while," Jocelyn said. "I think I'll go and stay at mother's house this week while they're gone. I don't like finding that man at my house. What about the lawsuit? Will you fight it?"

Austin looked so tired. Jocelyn had never seen him so vulnerable, so defeated.

"I don't know," he said. "That seems to be my answer for everything lately. What can I do? Civil suits can go on forever. You don't really fight them, you just try to defend yourself and minimize the damages. It could be very expensive, no matter what I do. I have a little money saved, and some investments. I could sell the house."

"I could sell mine," offered Jocelyn. "In fact, Gerald says someone wants to buy it right now. He gave me a business card with the guy's name. The place has to be worth something, the way land is being bought up—" She stopped abruptly, shocked at her own insight.

"It's the land," she said. "Folkert never wanted me to model for him. He wasn't trying to seduce me or compromise me in any way. He just wanted me to leave, like Mr. Vanderlaan, and the people on the other side. He thought if he was a big enough nuisance, I would bail out. And why not? I have no family, no roots there, no money. Now he's making veiled threats, and he's filed this suit against you. If he can't get me to move through intimidation, he'll force me to sell to raise the cash to help you. He knows I would do it. He wants the land. That's all he's ever wanted."

Austin frowned in concentration. "It's possible," he said. "I played right into his trap when I filed charges against him. It couldn't have been more convenient for him."

"But why didn't he just make an offer to buy?" asked Jocelyn. "He knew I needed money."

"But did Mr. Vanderlaan and the others? There's some reason why he wants all the property on the street vacated. He must know Greta will be moving. Let's find out if someone has made her parents an offer on the place."

"I'll go and call them," said Jocelyn. "I have their phone

number at home. Greta gave it to me for emergencies."
Jocelyn put her face in her hands. "The wedding is only
three days away! This is terrible."

"Jocelyn, we have to talk," Austin said, still with his
eyes closed and head back. "I want to talk about what's
happening to us. But I can't. . ." His voice trailed off. "I'm
so tired."

"I'm leaving now," Jocelyn whispered. "When is the
detective coming?"

Austin's lips barely moved. "Three o'clock."

"I'll be back," she said.

"Jocelyn."

"What?"

"Happy birthday."

She covered her mouth to muffle a sob. "How did you
know?"

"Driver's license, that first day. Come back at three."

She touched his cheek, then went outside, carefully
locking the door behind her, and sat in her car and cried.
That he would remember her birthday, and through his
pain let her know that he was thinking of her, nearly overwhelmed her. She managed to stop crying, and drove to
her mother's house.

Jocelyn called Greta at work to let her know what had
happened to Austin.

"He's going to be all right," said Jocelyn in response to
Greta's frightened shriek. "He's planning on standing up
with Randolph. He has a couple of days to recover. He
might not be quite as handsome as we'd like, but he'll be
there. You know Austin. You can count on him."

"Jocelyn, I'm just sick about you two calling off the wedding," said Greta. "I feel so guilty going ahead with mine."

"Well, stop," said Jocelyn. "Austin and I are just glad you and Randolph took the time to get to know each other a little better before walking down the aisle. Is he really everything you thought he would be?"

"And more," gushed Greta, "and just wait until you meet his family. They're all farmers! They can't understand why Randolph didn't want to spend his life in the dairy business, but they've decided it's all right, especially since they get free haircuts."

"I'm staying at my mother's house," said Jocelyn. She was about to tell Greta more of the details, but decided against it. "Hey, did Gerald Folkert ever offer to buy your parents' house?" asked Jocelyn.

"Folkert? That creep who lives on the hill just past your place? I spoke to him once. He came around asking if he could test our well. He passed himself off as some government worker, took a water sample, poured some chemical in it and said we were all going to die if we didn't get off that land in the next two months. That was just before my folks went to Florida. I called the county about it. They said it was a scam. When he came back, I threatened to have him arrested."

"But now your folks plan to sell."

"Well, sure, they don't want to move back here and I'm leaving. What's the matter? Is he giving you trouble?"

"I think he's giving a lot of people trouble," said Jocelyn. "I'm going to tell the police what he said to you, so don't be scared if they call."

"All right, but I'm leaving for Chicago tomorrow. I still have some things to do before the wedding."

"Don't forget, I'm coming in on the bus the morning of the wedding. I'll ride home with Austin," said Jocelyn. "I'm thinking of wearing my blue plaid shirt and jeans, all right?"

"I know you're joking," laughed Greta. "Are you joking? Don't you have a dress yet?"

"Don't be silly," said Jocelyn. "Of course I do. I'm wearing the one I wore in mother's wedding." The old saying echoed in her mind: *Always a bridesmaid, never a bride.*

Now, at last, Jocelyn had time to think, and to pray. She had discovered that Aunt Bebe's samplers held deep and wonderful truths that now made sense to her. The verses from the Bible were just the icing on the cake, she had learned. There were great depths of wisdom to be plumbed between the covers of the large, black book, its pages softened by her great-aunt's touch over the years. Jocelyn had found the Bible shortly after she moved into the house. At that time, she had wondered why it was so important to Bebe. Now she realized that its contents had governed every aspect of the woman's life, from business decisions and personal relationships to world philosophy and private worship. It was her secret of contentment, her guidebook. Jocelyn had begun reading it, taking special note of the handwritten messages Bebe had added in the margins.

Jocelyn had brought the KJV Bible along with her and opened it to read for a while. She came across Ephesians 4:28. "Let him that stole steal no more: but rather let him labour, working with his hands the thing which is good, that he may have to give to him that needeth." Next to the verse, Bebe had written, "Produce a product, offer a service; everyone has what he needs."

Jocelyn did not understand how the verse could be true. She had worked hard. Though unusual, her business was honest and met a need among advertisers and promoters. Why, then, was she so broke? Why had she received a windfall unrelated to her effort?

Throughout the day, she wrestled with the question, but came to no satisfactory answer before it was time to meet with the detective. She did not call her mother. *Let them honeymoon in peace,* she thought.

≈

"There's something going on," said Detective Dykema. "We sent a patrolman out to that construction site to ask about the car. We might get an answer on that from some of the workers. We'll be in touch." He took the business card Jocelyn had gotten from Gerald Folkert and left.

"I'm going to cook for you," said Jocelyn when the detective was gone. She went to Austin's immaculate kitchen and opened the refrigerator. It was nearly as empty as her own.

"Why don't you have any groceries?" she demanded. "You haven't been broke nearly as long as I have."

"I buy meat and vegetables the same day I plan to use them," said Austin. "Soup will be fine. There are several cans in the cupboard next to the range."

Austin noisily sipped the soup past his swollen lips. "Thank you," he said. "I haven't eaten anything all day. I feel better now."

There was little more to say. Jocelyn washed the bowls and announced she was leaving.

"I have a gift for you," said Austin. "I had planned to take you to dinner and then give it to you, but it didn't work out that way. I apologize. It hasn't been much of a birthday, especially for your twenty-first."

"It doesn't matter," Jocelyn replied, but Austin was walking toward his desk. She noticed how he sometimes caught his breath, and knew his cracked ribs were causing him pain.

From his desk drawer, Austin took a small, flat package wrapped in glossy blue paper with a silver bow.

"It reminds me of the outfit you wore at our cookout dinner," he said as he handed it to her. "I'm afraid it's a bit on the practical side, but hopefully not too much."

Jocelyn opened the package to find a set of delicately made pens engraved in gold with her name. There was also a holder made of black marble with gold fittings.

"I thought they might be useful in your work," Austin said.

Jocelyn nodded. "Yes, I do a lot of writing." She thought of the dozens of cheap pens she had used up in the past year. The check she was carrying around in her wallet suddenly seemed like an albatross about her neck. She knew what she had to do. Kissing Austin on the cheek, she said, "It's the perfect gift, Austin. It's exactly what I need."

Jocelyn drove to her mother's home and went to the tidy desk where her mother did correspondence. Jocelyn took out the new pen.

"This will be the first use I make of this gift," she said half-aloud, "because a gift is something entirely different than wages. They should not be confused."

Jocelyn got out a piece of plain white stationery and wrote to the publisher of the *Prizewinner's Bulletin*. "I cannot accept the check for your annual drawing," she wrote. "I did nothing to earn this money. It is contrary to my personal work ethic. Thanks, but no thanks." She put the note and the check into an envelope and quickly sealed it before she had a chance to change her mind. She found the stamps in the desk drawer, put one on the envelope, and started out to put it in the mailbox. As she was leaving, she caught sight of a large envelope with her name on it on a side table in the office.

Jocelyn absently picked up the envelope, remembering that her mother had mentioned leaving her the phone numbers and hotel and travel information for the trip. Jocelyn knew she was still not ready to call, however, and put the envelope into her purse.

It's simply a matter of trust, Jocelyn decided, as she lay staring at the ceiling that night. The money had come to her not to keep, but to reveal what it was she really needed—an understanding of who was in control of her life, and that He would bring about His plan in His time. He did not need the paltry contributions of contestants, which to Jocelyn now seemed like undeserved charity. She had always had what she needed, if not exactly what she wanted. She would continue to work. God would continue to supply. When that order changed, she decided, then it would be time for her to make some other choice.

❧

It wasn't the police, but a young newspaper reporter on his first job with the weekly paper who unraveled the scheme. While questioning neighbors who were protesting the increased truck traffic on Greenwood Road, he uncovered the plan to buy up large tracts of land, and under the guise of preparing the site for home building, mine the sand and gravel. The story broke the day after Austin and Jocelyn had spoken to the detective.

"We've seen it happen in other townships," the supervisor was quoted as saying. "This could have succeeded, and made a lot of money for a few people at the expense of the neighborhood. The board is now looking at ways to prevent it happening in the future."

The sheriff's department almost simultaneously discovered the link between Gerald Folkert and the would-be developers, who planned to increase their profit through kickbacks on the sale of the sand and gravel to highway construction contractors on the east side of the state. Folkert's friends, it turned out, were low-level mobsters trying to make some fast money where they assumed law enforcement was less sophisticated. The vandalism, sabotaged well, and false water testing were all traced to Folkert, who quickly implicated the others.

"Actually, we've had our eye on him since you filed that complaint," said Detective Dykema. "When we saw that business card, we knew what was going on. We always suspect organized crime when someone's dabbling in pornography. Oh! Excuse me. I mean *art prints.*"

"I see you don't agree with the prosecuting attorney either," said Austin.

Dykema grinned. "Those of us who do the legwork sometimes have different ideas about what should be legal. Sorry we couldn't intervene quickly enough to save you the bruises. This could never have been settled without you and your girlfriend. You'll be happy to know that Folkert is dropping the civil suit. He doesn't want to use all his visitation time talking to his lawyer."

That night, Martin Van Doran called his son from New York. "I found a buyer for the bubble propeller toy," he said. "Tell Jocelyn I've named it the Joc-a-Whirl, after her."

"She'll be pleased," said Austin. "When are you and Adelle coming home?"

"We decided to stay a couple more days. We're having a lot of fun. Son, I want you to know that we are supremely happy. What about yourself?"

How much should I say? Austin wondered. *Should I tell Dad I've reneged on my commitment to Jocelyn, lost my job, gone broke, and been beaten up all in the past few days?*

"I'm struggling with some things. There have been a few problems. I'll work through it."

"How?" asked Martin. "Have you asked Jocelyn for her help?"

"Dad, don't start—"

"Don't lose that girl," Martin said. "She almost lost you because of her stubbornness. Don't you make the same mistake. No matter what has happened, you can work—"

"Work it out," Austin said along with his father. "That's one of her favorite lines, and I've picked up on it, too. Don't worry about us, Dad. Just be happy. I'm glad you called tonight, though. We'll be out of town tomorrow for Greta's wedding. I'm standing up with Randolph, and of course, Jocelyn is maid of honor."

"A wedding is a good time to get engaged," suggested Martin. "Believe me, life goes by in a hurry. Don't wait, Austin. Nothing you have to do right now is more important than cementing your relationship with Jocelyn."

"I'll tell Jocelyn you won't be back in town until after the weekend," said Austin.

The next day, Austin showered and shaved, taking stock of the facial injuries as he viewed himself in the mirror. The swelling had subsided, and he figured those who did not know him would just think his face was naturally lopsided. He was happy not to have lost any teeth, and happy that he would have a few more days to heal before Martin and Adelle saw him.

As Austin looked at his face, now stripped of the camouflage that represented so many conflicts in his life, he wondered if starting again might not be as simple as shaving. Each day, make a fresh start. Jocelyn had said that after the pool party. He had been happy to do it then. Maybe she was ready, too.

Before he took his tuxedo from the closet, Austin went to his night table and picked up the gift he had gotten Jocelyn for her birthday but had not given to her. He decided to take it along, and trust God to work out the details.

The simple, elegant wedding with a few family members and friends belied the amount of effort Greta had put into the planning. When it was over, and the bride and groom had been safely sent on their weekend honeymoon, Austin and Jocelyn were left with the prospect of sharing the three-hour ride home with very little to say to each other.

As the city faded behind them and the sun began to set behind the high, wooded dunes along the Lake Michigan shoreline, Austin finally broke the silence.

"What do you think?" he asked. "Will it last? Between Greta and Randolph, I mean."

"I suppose it will, if they make it last," she said. "Hasn't this been strange? First, our parents—who turned out to be old friends—get married, and now Greta and Randolph, who are practically strangers. Yet both of them have the same opportunity for happiness."

"And you and I?" Austin asked, staring straight ahead at the unfolding highway, and feeling his heart thump in his chest. Jocelyn was silent for what seemed far too long, and Austin continued, "I know what I think—or, I should say, what I *believe*. I believe circumstances don't change anything. I love you as much as I did when you were poor. I love you as much as I did before we were in danger. I love you as much—no, *more* than I did when I thought I was king of the hill. I love you, Jocelyn. I want you to marry me. You said yes once, but then I valued my own pride more than your love. Forgive me, Jocelyn. Marry me."

"Stop the car," Jocelyn said.

"What's wrong?" he asked, quickly pulling to the side of the highway. The orange sunset cast its glow over the sandy oak-studded flats east of the shoreline. There were no houses in sight, and hardly any passing vehicles. If Jocelyn was carsick, Austin was unsure what he would do. He waited anxiously.

"Do you really love me, rich or poor?" asked Jocelyn. "I mean, if *you* are rich or poor. What if someone else files a lawsuit, like the owner of some dog that you kicked out of the way? Or me. What if I come into even more big winnings?"

Austin looked confused. "What do you mean? That has nothing to do with my love for you."

"Or what if I try some other business after we're married and bankrupt us? Would you still love me?"

Austin hesitated a moment. He was beginning to understand. "Jocelyn, what I've learned is that we have to trust

God each day. Life can't be predicted, and love doesn't happen by chance. I plan to love you. I control that decision. Now, will you answer me?"

"I told you once," she said. "Yes, I'll marry you." She stretched across the seat to put her arms around his neck. "I have to tell you something, though. I gave back the money."

"What money? The money from the magazine? The $247,000?"

Jocelyn nodded. "I couldn't keep it. I didn't feel it was rightfully mine, not like the winnings from contests I entered. I couldn't let you go on thinking I was rich."

"I'm rich," he said. "I'm the richest man alive. Here, I want to give you the birthday gift I bought for you several weeks ago, but couldn't give it to you." From the glove box, Austin pulled the package he had brought along and handed it to Jocelyn. Inside was a diamond engagement ring. He slipped it on her finger.

Jocelyn sighed. "Let's go home," she said. "Should we call the folks, or tell them when they get home?"

"My dad let me know his opinion of the rift between us," he said. "I'd call him right now on the cellular if I had the phone number."

Jocelyn opened her purse. "I think I put that list in here that mother left for me." She pulled out the envelope and began looking at the papers inside.

"This isn't their itinerary like I thought it was," she said. "It's some kind of legal stuff." She continued to read, a puzzled look on her face, handing Austin the pages as she finished.

"Jocelyn, I hate to tell you this, but I think you're rich again. Not terribly rich, just comfortably set. Your father left money for you that you are to receive now—after your twenty-first birthday."

"I didn't know about any money," said Jocelyn. "I used to get an allowance, but I made Mother stop sending it to me."

"I'd say it was all from the same trust—an allowance until you were twenty-one, and then the principal pays out after that," Austin concluded. "I'd also say she intended to talk this over with you when she had some indication you were ready to accept it."

"I can't stand it," Jocelyn murmured, and slumped into the seat. "Engaged, not engaged. Rich, not rich—then rich again. Threatened, safe. What's going to happen tomorrow?"

"Tomorrow?" Austin asked. "Tomorrow, I am going to continue to love you, and we will trust God for the strength to deal with whatever He sends."

epilogue

July, one year later

Jocelyn stood by the mailbox wearing an old pair of jean cutoffs and a faded T-shirt that said "Property of U.S. Air Force" on the back. In the distance, she could see a mail truck coming down the road.

"Hi, Whitney," she said, when the truck finally stopped. "I am so glad you're back on this route."

"I hated the city," said Whitney, handing Jocelyn a stack of envelopes. "Lucky for you I made the transfer when I did, though. How's Austin?"

"Happy as a king. Come over to the boutique this week. I'm having a special sale on hats. I've got one that will be perfect with that sundress you bought a couple of weeks ago."

"I love shopping at your vintage clothing store. Are you sure you don't miss your contest business?"

Jocelyn shook her head. "I love the shop. Everyone who comes in is excited about the place. Why did I think I could shut myself away from people and be happy? I just chose the wrong business."

"Well, you still got yourself a winner," said Whitney, and drove away.

Jocelyn walked across the road to the renovated farmhouse, the landscaped yard, and large herb gardens, now immaculately cultivated. The sign above the front porch said "Van Doran Landscape Design."

"Mrs. Van Doran," said Austin, as he met her at the door. "Are you tampering with the mail? Don't you know that's a crime?"

Jocelyn continued looking through the envelopes. "Well, you never know what kind of offer might come in the mail," she declared, slowly brushing past him. "It never hurts to look."

"Oh?" he said, taking her in his arms. "Are you looking for something better?"

Jocelyn smiled up at her husband, placed her hands on his cheeks, and kissed him. "This is the grand prize," she announced. "It doesn't get any better."

A Letter To Our Readers

Dear Reader:

In order that we might better contribute to your reading enjoyment, we would appreciate your taking a few minutes to respond to the following questions. We welcome your comments and read each form and letter we receive. When completed, please return to the following:

Rebecca Germany, Fiction Editor
Heartsong Presents
PO Box 719
Uhrichsville, Ohio 44683

1. Did you enjoy reading *Prize Package?*
   ❑ Very much. I would like to see more books
      by this author!
   ❑ Moderately
      I would have enjoyed it more if _____
      _____
      _____

2. Are you a member of **Heartsong Presents**? Yes ❑ No❑
   If no, where did you purchase this book?_____
   _____

3. How would you rate, on a scale from 1 (poor) to 5 (superior), the cover design?_____

4. On a scale from 1 (poor) to 10 (superior), please rate the following elements.

   _____ Heroine   _____ Plot

   _____ Hero   _____ Inspirational theme

   _____ Setting   _____ Secondary characters

5. These characters were special because_____

_____

_____

6. How has this book inspired your life?_____

_____

_____

7. What settings would you like to see covered in future **Heartsong Presents** books?_____

_____

_____

8. What are some inspirational themes you would like to see treated in future books?_____

_____

_____

9. Would you be interested in reading other **Heartsong Presents** titles?   Yes ❑   No ❑

10. Please check your age range:
    ❑ Under 18   ❑ 18-24   ❑ 25-34
    ❑ 35-45   ❑ 46-55   ❑ Over 55

11. How many hours per week do you read?_____

Name _____

Occupation _____

Address _____

City _____ State _____ Zip _____

Ah, those homemade,

comforting family dinners around the table. But who has time to make them between carpooling and softball games?

Don't let your busy schedule deter you. This collection of delectable recipes—from the readers and authors of inspirational romances—has been gathered from all over the United States, and even from Greece and Australia.

There are tried and true recipes for every occasion— Crock-Pot meals for busy days, fast desserts for church dinners, rave snacks for after school, holiday gifts for those picky relatives, and much, much more. Over 700 recipes await you! Bring back the joy of treasured moments over good food with the ones you love. So, dust off the china and treat your loved ones (and yourself) to some delicious home cooking.

The Heart's Delight *cookbook has what every family needs—cooking from the heart.*

400 pages, Paperbound, 8" x 5 ³⁄₁₆"

·····Heartsong·····

CONTEMPORARY ROMANCE IS CHEAPER BY THE DOZEN!

Any 12 Heartsong Presents titles for only $26.95 **

Buy any assortment of twelve Heartsong Presents titles and save 25% off of the already discounted price of $2.95 each!

**plus $1.00 shipping and handling per order and sales tax where applicable.

HEARTSONG PRESENTS *TITLES AVAILABLE NOW:*

_HP149 LLAMA LAND, *VeraLee Wiggins*
_HP177 NEPALI NOON, *Susannah Hayden*
_HP178 EAGLES FOR ANNA, *Cathrine Runyon*
_HP181 RETREAT TO LOVE, *Nancy N. Rue*
_HP182 A WING AND A PRAYER, *Tracie J. Peterson*
_HP185 ABIDE WITH ME, *Una McManus*
_HP186 WINGS LIKE EAGLES, *Tracie J. Peterson*
_HP189 A KINDLED SPARK, *Colleen L. Reece*
_HP190 A MATTER OF FAITH, *Nina Coombs Pykare*
_HP193 COMPASSIONATE LOVE, *Ann Bell*
_HP197 EAGLE PILOT, *Jill Stengl*
_HP198 WATERCOLOR CASTLES, *Ranee McCollum*
_HP201 A WHOLE NEW WORLD, *Yvonne Lehman*
_HP202 SEARCH FOR TODAY, *Mary Hawkins*
_HP205 A QUESTION OF BALANCE, *Veda Boyd Jones*
_HP206 POLITICALLY CORRECT, *Kay Cornelius*
_HP209 SOFT BEATS MY HEART, *Aleesha Carter*
_HP210 THE FRUIT OF HER HANDS, *Jane Orcutt*
_HP213 PICTURE OF LOVE, *Tamela Hancock Murray*

_HP214 TOMORROW'S RAINBOW, *VeraLee Wiggins*
_HP217 ODYSSEY OF LOVE, *Melanie Panagiotopoulos*
_HP218 HAWAIIAN HEARTBEAT, *Yvonne Lehman*
_HP221 THIEF OF MY HEART, *Catherine Bach*
_HP222 FINALLY, LOVE, *Jill Stengl*
_HP225 A ROSE IS A ROSE, *Ruth Richert Jones*
_HP226 WINGS OF THE DAWN, *Tracie J. Peterson*
_HP229 TREASURE OF THE KEYS, *Stephen A. Papuchis*
_HP230 AFTERGLOW, *Irene B. Brand*
_HP233 FAITH CAME LATE, *Freda Chrisman*
_HP234 GLOWING EMBERS, *Colleen L. Reece*
_HP237 THE NEIGHBOR, *Debra Whitesmith*
_HP238 ANNIE'S SONG, *Andrea Boeshaar*
_HP241 DESTINY, ARIZONA, *Marty Crisp*
_HP242 FAR ABOVE RUBIES, *Becky Melby and Cathy Wienke*
_HP245 CROSSROADS, *Tracie Peterson and Jennifer Peterson*
_HP246 BRIANNA'S PARDON, *Gloria Clover*
_HP249 MOUNTAINTOP, *Lauralee Bliss*
_HP250 SOMETHING FROM NOTHING, *Nancy Lavo*

(If ordering from this page, please remember to include it with the order form.)

Presents

Great Inspirational Romance at a Great Price!

Heartsong Presents books are inspirational romances in contemporary and historical settings, designed to give you an enjoyable, spirit-lifting reading experience. You can choose wonderfully written titles from some of today's best authors like Veda Boyd Jones, Yvonne Lehman, Tracie Peterson, Debra White Smith, and many others.

When ordering quantities less than twelve, above titles are $2.95 each.
Not all titles may be available at time of order.

Hearts♥ng Presents
Love Stories Are Rated G!

That's for godly, gratifying, and of course, great! If you love a thrilling love story, but don't appreciate the sordidness of some popular paperback romances, **Heartsong Presents** is for you. In fact, **Heartsong Presents** is the *only inspirational romance book club*, the only one featuring love stories where Christian faith is the primary ingredient in a marriage relationship.

Sign up today to receive your first set of four, never before published Christian romances. Send no money now; you will receive a bill with the first shipment. You may cancel at any time without obligation, and if you aren't completely satisfied with any selection, you may return the books for an immediate refund!

Imagine. . .four new romances every four weeks—two historical, two contemporary—with men and women like you who long to meet the one God has chosen as the love of their lives. . .all for the low price of $9.97 postpaid.

To join, simply complete the coupon below and mail to the address provided. **Heartsong Presents** romances are rated G for another reason: They'll arrive *Godspeed!*
